ary Media Center
Carroll Community College
1601 Washington Road
Westminster, Maryland 21157

WITHDRAWN

TRAP DOORS AND TROJAN HORSES

by
Iris Weil Collett
and
Lawrence Murphy Smith

Auditing is a systematic process of objectively obtaining and evaluating evidence regarding assertions about economic actions and events to ascertain the degree of correspondence between the assertions and established criteria and communicating the results to interested users.
— Committee on Basic Accounting Concepts
American Accounting Association

D1225667

Cover photograph, ATLANTA SKYLINE,
by Deborah William Hirshman

TRAP DOORS AND TROJAN HORSES is fiction, and all the
charaters and adventures are imaginary. Any resemblance
to actual persons, living or dead, is purely coincidental.

Dedicated to
Paul "loose cannon" Biddle
and Mary Katherine "Guts" Taken

Copyright © 1991 Thomas Horton and Daughters

No part of this work may be reproduced in any
form without permission in writing from the publisher.

Library of Congress Catalog Card Number 89-81733

ISBN 0-913878-45-6

TRAP DOORS AND TROJAN HORSES

Lenny Cramer is back! The famous forensic accountant has joined the accounting faculty at Georgia State University. In addition to his professorial duties he is conducting an operational audit for the world famous soft drink company, Coca-Cola. Intrigue and fraud place Lenny's life on the line as he uncovers a scheme to steal Coke's secret formula. The story features a variety of settings, from Atlanta to Washington, D.C. to Poland. In addition to his auditing and teaching duties, Professor Cramer testifies before a Congressional hearing concerning the integrity of the accounting profession and in an Atlanta courtroom as an expert witness on auditing and statistical sampling. With his assistant, Slam Duncan, an accounting Ph.D. student, he puts state-of-the-art technology to work to solve audit problems.

Preface

This supplementary text may be used near the end of an auditing or beginning of a data processing course. It would be ideal for an MBA program that has a light coverage of accounting. It could be used in CPA firms' in-house training programs. This novel illustrates the differences between a regular audit and the investigation required by forensic accountants to uncover computer fraud. It should be read by every business executive.

The novel mixes fraud, crime, politics, and auditing for a better and easier way to learn accounting. If used as a supplement to an auditing course or a computer course, this exciting novel provides a painless way of learning auditing principles. The suspenseful story combines computer and auditing concepts in a fashion even a novice can understand and enjoy. With computer fraud losses reaching $3 billion per year according to Ernst & Young, accountants must be familiar with computer auditing.

Professor Lenny Cramer operates a small forensic accounting firm in Atlanta, Georgia. As a forensic accountant, he goes beyond recordkeeping and looks at the records to learn and gather information. Called "a sort of Indiana Jones of the Ledger Set" by the *Washington Post*, Lenny testifies before Congressional committees and serves as an expert witness in the courtroom. In *Trap Doors and Trojan Horses*, he and his sidekick, Slam Duncan, investigate a mysterious series of computer losses at a division of Coca-Cola. Coke, of course, is one of the world's most popular and best recognized consumer products.

Cramer and Duncan employ auditing and computer concepts in making real-life decisions. Along the way, business practices, political controversies, contemporary individual and corporate planning, accounting fraud, and the lives of CPAs and their colleagues are elucidated in a way both students and instructors will find gripping and informative. This instructive and entertaining approach is an excellent substitute for a mundane practice set. The novel shows accounting students that the accounting profession is much better than the stereotype image most people have. An effective accountant is bright, personable, and technically competent.

The authors acknowledge the work on the early chapters by Hugh Nations. The authors are grateful to following people for their review and comments on earlier versions of the novel: Barbara Apostolou, Teresa Conover, James C. Flagg, Steve Flory, David Kerr, R. Stephen McDuffie, Alfred R. Michenzi, Jeffrey R. Miller, Barbara Morris, Winston T. Shearon, Katherine T. Smith, Robert Strawser, and James H. Thompson. Any shortcomings, however, remain the total responsibility of the authors.

> By focusing on protagonists like the forensic accountant—the investigator of ledgers—a novel allows the otherwise dry accounting material to take on the aura of mystery. The dramatic intrigue, in turn, helps the reader retain the principles.
>
> The Administrator

Coca-Cola and Coke are registered trademarks. Most trademarks do not have definitely determinable useful lives, and the direct consideration paid for an intangible asset cannot be amortized.

All characters, other than purely historical characters, and events in this book are fictitious, and any resemblance to actual persons and events is coincidental.

TRAP DOORS AND TROJAN HORSES
Chapter 1

Man is the only animal who drinks when he isn't thirsty.
— Mark Twain

Lenny Cramer could feel the grip of nagging tension relaxing its hold just the slightest as he drank his Cherry Coke. It brought back boyhood memories. The flavor was slightly reminiscent of the Cherry Cokes he used to drink at the soda fountain of his old neighborhood drugstore. He then thought about his new consulting job. He was rather pleased that the Coca Cola Company had hired him. After all, Coke was a major international business firm. It was one of the 30 companies included in the Dow Jones Industrial Average, the stock market barometer. The thought of working for the company that manufactured his beverage made each sip particularly refreshing.

He and his daughter were now residing in Atlanta, the queen city of the South. As he thought about his new home, Cramer began recalling scenes from the epic motion picture, *Gone With The Wind*. Cramer had a passion for history and had read numerous books about the Civil War. As wars go, it was an exceptionally tragic one. Families were divided by the conflict. Even President and Mrs. Lincoln had family members fighting on each side. The city of Atlanta was burned to the ground by the Union forces under General William Tecumseh Sherman. For many years, people with the surname of Sherman felt a little uncomfortable living in Georgia.

Cramer looked at his daughter and mused with a twinge of regret. Rebecca soon would be partaking of all the joys that adulthood holds —

1

independence, self-reliance, marriage, children; not to mention, mortgages, ulcers, traffic jams, income taxes, and the daily grind. At 14, Rebecca was already beginning to show the promise of exuberant womanhood. The nose was a trifle long, a legacy from the Cramer side of the family that immediately stamped them as father and daughter, but the wide-set eyes gave her an air of constant crinkling delighted surprise that Cramer knew would one day devastate the young men who crossed her path. His late wife hadn't been beautiful, but he had counted himself lucky to win her over the many suitors who, like himself, had fallen into those same eyes and found themselves snared. Watching Rebecca as she had walked away to the ladies' room, Cramer had felt a warm envy for his daughter's next 10 or 12 years. Adolescence and college and just getting started in his profession had been some of the most exciting years of his life, he reflected. And he suspected Rebecca would fit right into the Southern ambiance, despite her initial reluctance at leaving Philadelphia.

Just now, Cramer himself was feeling a trifle uncomfortable, and after a moment he finally was able to identify the source. It was the atmosphere in the lobby bar at the Peachtree Plaza. Well ... not the atmosphere so much as the surroundings.

On his earlier visits to the Georgia capital, Cramer had stayed at the Hyatt Regency. The Peachtree Plaza was much newer than the Regency, and the lobby bar was one of the city's showcases. The tables were virtually islands set in an indoor lagoon, and being surrounded by so much water was having its effect. Cramer felt an unmistakable urge to visit the men's room, though he knew it wasn't really necessary. The professor smiled as he reflected that the same urge had probably been what nudged Rebecca to the ladies room.

The Peachtree Plaza was an extravagant edifice—tallest hotel in the nation, and the view from the Sun Dial, the revolving bar atop the 74-story hotel was without parallel in the city. Rebecca and he had visited the Sun Dial briefly last night, just long enough for each to have a soft drink. Cramer had been even more uneasy then, and it had nothing to do with his kidneys. He just didn't like being stuck that high up, with no way to get down in the event of a fire.

Cramer had to admit, however, that the view from the bar was worth the visit. Patrons could follow the course of world-famed Peachtree Street as it wound northward for miles through the city toward the affluent Sandy Springs and Roswell area. Looking out on the panorama, Cramer had even been able to point out the imposing granite bulk of Stone Mountain to the east.

Just as the Peachtree Plaza was an architectural extravagance, Cramer thought—this stay was an extravagance for him as well. On earlier visits, he had chosen more modest accommodations. But this time Rebecca was along for her introduction to her new home, and Cramer wanted to make it special for her. God knows she's been through enough in the past year, he recollected, even if he did try to shield her from as much as possible. Still, he knew there had been incidents: some things had been said by Rebecca's classmates at Englehurst, and some of her playmates no longer came around after the trouble at Wharton. She'd borne it well, but Cramer knew his sensitive daughter well enough to know that his troubles had left their marks. The move to Atlanta should prove a God-send, Cramer mused, even if Rebecca wasn't crazy about the idea initially. It would be a little rough at the beginning starting all over again in a new city. "If I could get through the past year, though, I should be able to do just about anything," he thought.

"Miss Simondson used to call my musing wool gathering when I did it in class. She'd always ask, 'Are you planning to knit an Afghan when you're through?'"

Rebecca's throaty voice pulled Cramer back from his reverie. He smiled inwardly: More than once, women of his acquaintance who had not met Rebecca had greeted him frostily after Rebecca answered the phone. Only after they learned that the voice was his adolescent daughter had their tone thawed. It was a marvel, that voice, coming as it did from a youngster who stood less than five feet tall and who couldn't decide yet which was more exciting, tennis or boys. Quickly, Cramer put away any thoughts of women. That did nothing but evoke thoughts of the last time he had seen Dana, his close friend clad in prison gray, her face drawn but still defiantly beautiful.

"Just thinking about all we have to do this week, Honey," Cramer replied. "We've got to move in when the van comes tomorrow, and then we must get the house in order. Of course, I must do the same with the office. We're going to be pretty busy for a few days, so I guess we'd better enjoy ourselves tonight. I forgot to tell you, Will and Emma want us to come over for dinner Friday night."

"I'd like that," Rebecca said. "How long has it been since I've seen them? Years and years. I remember the last time. They gave me Artemis. You're not going to tell them what happened to him, are you?"

Artemis was a stuffed lamb that the Poseys had given Becc. A smile flickered briefly across Cramer's face as he remembered how his wife, who hated nicknames, had insisted that if her daughter was going to have to suffer through life with one, it wouldn't be something mundane like Becky. Their one visit to Philadelphia had, indeed, been years ago, and it had been a grand reunion of two old friends. It seemed they'd relived almost every one of their moments at Harvard, where both had earned MBAs. Cramer had been on the top of the heap at the time of that visit: a Distinguished Professor at Wharton, almost a sure shot for an accounting chair at the next vacancy, and a lucrative consulting business in auditing on the side.

Then the long nightmare had begun. For a time, it appeared that he would lose his Certified Public Accountant (CPA) certificate, and would face the ultimate humiliation of being reported in the semi-monthly *The CPA Letter* that he had been expelled from the accounting profession that he loved. But the plagiarizing charge that had begun his long fall into desolation had been proved false. If he had ever doubted it, Cramer at least had the satisfaction of knowing now that he practiced in a profession where ethics meant something.

The codes of the American Institute of CPAs and of the various state societies had teeth. However, even if he had been expelled or suspended from both the Pennsylvania Society of CPAs and the AICPA, he could still have practiced accounting—if he were able to find clients. Both organizations were voluntary societies. Only if the Pennsylvania Board of Accountancy had suspended or revoked his CPA certificate, which was effectively his union card, would he have lost his right to practice accounting.

But that hadn't happened. That numbing episode was all behind now, and it was Will, with his undistinguished but stable job in the overseas development arm of Coca-Cola, who had come to his rescue after Cramer's troubles had cost him his position and his standing in the accounting profession. Good old solid, plodding Will, who'd wrangled his new teaching post at Georgia State University for the fall, who had found him the small bungalow he and Rebecca would be renting, and who owned the small office building where Cramer would set up shop. Will had already gotten him his first commission, a small auditing job at the Coca-Cola division where Will worked.

Ernst & Young was Coke's independent auditor who performed their yearly financial statement audit. The purpose of a financial state-ment audit is to provide an opinion of the fairness of the statements, as to conformity with generally accepted accounting principles. Will wanted Cramer to perform an operational audit without the word getting out to many people. It wasn't exactly hush-hush, as Cramer understood it, but Will did want the project kept quiet. The job was small potatoes compared to the not-so-distant days when Cramer was a consultant to major international corporations, but Cramer was grateful both for the work and for the confidence his friend had shown in him.

"We'd better get started if we're going to take in everything at Stone Mountain before the light show tonight," Cramer told his daughter as he beckoned for the check. The two had planned to take in the huge granite mountain east of Atlanta as their one day of fun before buckling down for a couple of weeks of getting their new home into shape. Atlanta's other attractions—the Cyclorama, zoo, the High Museum, the state Capitol—would have to wait till later. But Cramer wanted to give his daughter at least a taste of the delights the Southern metropolis held, and Stone Mountain seemed to be the best way to do that.

His judgment turned out to be eminently correct. After a day of oggling the huge carving of Southern heroes Robert E. Lee, Stonewall Jackson, and Jefferson Davis that graced the side of the mountain, riding the train, visiting the game ranch and old car museum, and ooh-ing at the laser light show, the two returned to the hotel that night tired but enthusiastic over what their new home held in store. Cramer was amused and grateful, but just a little wistful, when he noticed how much Becc's attitude toward the move improved when she met a group of teenage boys at the Stone Mountain park lake, where they relaxed with a dip in the cool water for an hour or two.

"I guess a parent hasn't done his job right if he doesn't eventually render himself unnecessary," Cramer mused before he drifted off to sleep. "But that doesn't make it any easier."

*　　*　　*

The next few days were a blur of scrubbing, sweeping, vacuuming, mopping, waxing, washing windows, moving furniture, moving it back again, hanging pictures, painting, mowing, pulling weeds, and all the other multitudinous tasks involved in setting up housekeeping. The bungalow had been unoccupied for the past year and half, while it was tied up in an estate, and the long vacancy showed. Southern cobwebs seemed to flourish more than their Northern cousins, Cramer noted. Rebecca worked right beside him without complaining, but Cramer knew it was an inauspicious introduction to her new home, and he made it a point to give her frequent breaks while he himself kept plugging away.

The house was smaller than either he or Becc were accustomed to, and Cramer didn't care much for the idea of renting. It wasn't that he couldn't afford to buy. Cramer was far from being on the dole. But

5

with the uncertainties of starting a new firm in a new city, he thought it best to husband his resources for a year or two. Besides, he wanted the opportunity to get to know Atlanta and environs before settling down in a permanent residence. There would be plenty of time to buy after the Philadelphia place sold. The tax code allows a homeowner two years to reinvest sale proceeds in another home before taxing any gain from the sale of a residence. Cramer figured that within that period he could find a place he and Rebecca could turn into a **real** home.

Several times, Cramer called a halt while he went to his nearby office. That, too, had to be shaped up, and Cramer didn't have the heart to ask Becc's help. The same van that had brought the Cramer household goods had brought enough of the furnishings from his former office in Philadelphia to equip the new quarters in Atlanta. Though he wasn't confronted with the same housecleaning chores that awaited him at home, Cramer still had to interview for a secretary, get his telephones hooked up, and unpack his library and electronic gear. The CPA had prided himself on having the best and latest in technology in Philadelphia, and he fully intended to adhere to that in Atlanta.

By the time Friday afternoon arrived, the house was sparkling and had begun to feel like a home, and the office was ready, expectantly waiting his arrival Monday morning. He and Rebecca knocked off, ready for the dinner with the Poseys and the weekend of visiting Atlanta attractions that Cramer had promised.

Cramer even had time to browse through the latest copy of *The Quantum PC Report for CPAs*. One article in particular caught his eye. The author, Steve Greenberg, contended that eventually every hard drive on a computer will fail, with the resultant loss of all the programs and data on it. Greenberg's solution was both obvious and simple: Make a copy, on a regular basis, of all the information on the drive.

The world sure would be better off, Cramer mused just before easing off into a short but well-deserved nap, if we'd all try the obvious, simple solutions to problems more frequently.

★ ★ ★

"Got the office all ship-shape? Ready to hit the ground running Monday?" Will Posey asked Cramer. The two old friends were relaxing in the den as his wife and Rebecca were cleaning up after a homecooked meal. The dinner had almost made Cramer wince at the memories of what he had lost when his wife died. As a cook she had been the equal of Emma Posey.

6

"Well, I'm ready to hit the ground, but I suspect it'll be at more of a trot than at a run," Cramer replied. "When a fellow reaches my age, the only time he runs is when something's chasing him."

"I know I've said this before, Will," Lenny continued, "but I do want you to know I appreciate everything you've done. If you hadn't been so insistent, I probably would have gone on moldering and moping in Philadelphia forever. I know you've gone out on a limb, and I'm grateful."

"Hey, I haven't done anything except to recommend that we hire the best CPA I know to do a little snooping for my division. You're a natural, one of the best experts around on forensic accounting and data processing."

"Well, I thought I met the first standard of the Generally Accepted Auditing Standards—competence. But after getting hoodwinked by Dana Scott, I sometimes wonder even about that," Cramer said wryly.

Posey brushed off his friend's protestations. "Love can blind anybody's judgment. How could you know that she would try to rip-off those diamonds in Rangoon? Besides, even CPAs have their professional escape hatches. Like they taught us, an ordinary audit is not primarily intended to detect fraud..."

"Unless the effect on the financial statements is material," Cramer interrupted. "At least I've got that down pat."

"Anyway, all it took was to bring the boss over one night and feed him one of Emma's pot roasts, and he was sold. Of course, I did have to hook a couple of shots at the club before we got home for dinner, but it was worth it to know you'll be getting off to a good start here."

"How do you like your new secretary? What's her name?"

"Michele Poe, and it looks like she'll be great. She just got tired of that 30-mile round trip into town every day, even if she had to take a pay cut to avoid the traffic jams. Traffic must really be a rascal here in Atlanta, if she's willing to give up a good job with Peat Marwick Main to come with me. She knows it will be a while before she'll be getting the salary and benefits she had with Peat. I read in the July/August issue of *Emerson's Professional Service Review* that Ernst & Young had vaulted to the top spot."

"Once you have the dubious opportunity to drive in Atlanta's 5 o'clock traffic, you'll understand why she feels that way. The only thing I can think of that's worse is being stuck in the Omni when one of those heavy metal groups is tearing the place up. Makes me just about as nervous as being tied up on the Northeast Expressway. What firms come after E&Y?"

"The piece lists Arthur Andersen second and Deloitte & Touche third. Those mergers in the late eighties shook-up the pack."

Posey frowned, "Let me fill you in, though, on what to expect at the office when you start giving us the famous Cramer Crunch. As you know, we're not expecting a full-scale financial statement audit. E&Y handles that, and does a fine job. But the boss thinks we need somebody to come in to make sure nothing really serious is going on. Here is a set of last year's financials."

"So what we're talking about is an operational audit," Cramer said, as he took the manila folder.

"C'mon, Lenny. You know how long it's been since I cracked a textbook. What's an operational audit?"

"It's a systematic review of the activities of a business, or of a stipulated segment of them, in relationship to specified objectives. It is an organized search for ways of improving efficiency and effectiveness," Cramer explained. "E&Y does your regular audit. They issue a written conclusion about the reliability of Coke's written assertions on your balance sheet, income statement, and other statements."

"I'm asking you to constructively criticize our accounting procedures and controls," Posey said airily. "Normally, all my division handles is the identification and initial development of overseas markets. It's up to us to keep up with what's going on around the globe, with an eye toward what will make a buck or two for Coke. Once a specified number of the citizens of an underdeveloped nation reach a given income level, for example, it's up to my folks to know about it, and try to take advantage of it by opening up the market for Coke. It's a little more complicated than that, however. We have to factor in population concentration, for example, and the number of urban centers, and cultural influences. Basically what it boils down to, though, is a numbers game. Oh, we also have to make sure that we haven't ticked off any banana republic prima donnas, or if we have, we have to sweet-talk them if it looks like maybe we want to set up a bottling plant on their front lawn."

"Internally, my division uses microcomputers for our housekeeping chores. But all of our demographics work is done on one of the company mainframes...that kind of data-shuffling requires a lot of horsepower. I'm not one of your whiz kids on computers, so if I'm not speaking the lingo right, just overlook it."

"What's happened is that something has come up that could be an embarrassment to the division—or at least to our divisional chief—in more ways than one." Posey frowned.

Posey thought for a moment and continued. "Joe's a good executive; I've never worked for any better. But he does have a problem maintaining high personal integrity. Here a little while back, he got involved with one of the women in the office; apparently it all started with some 'innocent' flirting which unfortunately led to something more serious. What made it even more stupid for Joe is that her husband works for the division, too. One day, she's really bent out of shape with her husband. He'd promised her a new car and bought a bass boat instead, and she tells Joe that the guy is using the computer to play songs it's not supposed to play."

"Exactly what, she wouldn't or couldn't say, but she did know he'd paid cash for that boat. The lady cashes her husband's paycheck, so she knew he shouldn't have that kind of money. The problem is, Joe can't confront the thing directly. The lady and her husband are back on great terms again.....close as two Irishmen with only one beer between 'em."

"So you suspect fraud," Cramer suggested.

"Furthermore," Posey continued, "there's another problem. Joe's on a fast track at the company, and he can't afford any kind of problems in his division that cause problems for other divisions. The mainframe we use is the one that handles the billings to all of our bottlers, along with several miscellaneous operations. Some of the canned juice billings, for example, are on the system, and have been for about two years. And it handles many of the accounts payable for several divisions. That's temporary. Ultimately, they're to be switched over to another part of the company, but the Syrup Set—that's what we call the other division that handles the syrup accounts—has got 'em for now."

"Who does the billings for the bottlers themselves?" Cramer asked. "Are those all franchises, or are some of them company-owned, and if they are, do they do their billing locally?"

"Hmmmmm...I forgot you're not an Atlantan," Posey smiled. "Coca-Cola—the Coca-Cola Company—does very little bottling. Let me give you some history."

"The first Coke bottler was Joseph Biedenharn, a soda fountain operator in Vicksburg, Mississippi. That was in 1894. Then in 1897, two lawyers in Chattanooga, Tennessee, persuaded Coca-Cola President Asa Candler to give them the rights to bottle and sell Coca-Cola throughout the United States, except for Mississippi, Texas, and five New England states. The lawyers were Benjamin Franklin Thomas and Joseph Brown Whitehead. They were the real beginning of the franchise system that dominated Coke for almost a century, and they got a bargain. They paid only one dollar for the bottling rights."

"That was the bargain of the century," Cramer commented.

"Yeah. They paid less than the cost of a two-liter bottle of Coke today. Coke's got one of the most interesting corporate histories around. It all began with an Atlanta pharmacist, John S. Pemberton. He registered a trademark for 'French Wine Cola - ideal nerve and tonic stimulant.' His first advertisement appeared in the Atlanta *Constitution* in May 1886—'Delicious and Refreshing.' The concoction was wine with—get this—cocaine. The next year Pemberton deleted the wine and added caffeine and a kola nut extract. He changed the name to Coca-Cola, and peddled it as 'brain food.' I remember one 1892 ad. It described Coke as 'The great brain and nerve tonic. Makes a pleasant and refreshing drink and is certain relief for some forms of headache.'"

"There are a lot of teenagers, including my own, who'll be glad to hear it's a brain tonic," Cramer chuckled.

"There's more," Posey continued. "Asa Candler was another guy who got a bargain with Coca-Cola. He was an Atlanta businessman, and in 1891 he bought all the rights to Coke from Pemberton for $2,300. Candler began selling the syrup to wholesalers, who sold it to drugstores to be mixed with carbonated water and sold at soda fountains. In 1919, the company was sold for $25 million. That's a return of about 10,870 percent in 28 years. I calculated it once. That comes out to a return of 388 percent per year. But as to the original point. Coca-Cola recently has been buying up its bottlers through a separate subsidiary called Coca-Cola Enterprises. Coke owns 49 percent of that operation. We're trying to consolidate. In 1950 there were more than a thousand bottlers. By 1985, they'd been reduced to 400, and we plan to continue to consolidate."

Posey shifted on the light blue couch and spoke again. "But let's get back to our immediate problem. What Joe is worried about most is Uncle Jemima. That's Jeremiah Mortimer Clifford II, who heads up the syrup crew. He and Joe go way back, which is where Uncle Jemima would like to send Joe. They're old college classmates, and there hasn't been a good feeling between them since Joe put a dead snake in Clifford's bed one night and Clifford actually wet his pants in front of half the Dartmouth lacrosse team. Joe's quite a one for pranks. Unfortunately, Clifford's even bigger on grudges than Joe is on pranks. He'd love to nail Joe's hide to the office door of the vice president for operations."

"That's why, *if* there's any hanky-panky going on with the computers, Joe's got to get a fix on it first. That way he not only can head off Uncle Jemima, but he can actually come out looking good...like he's on top of things."

"I'll do my best," Cramer promised.

"That's always been good enough for me," Will replied. "C'mon, let's go bore the girls with more of the old college days. And for goodness sake, don't mention that episode with Cathy Olfers when we were first-year graduate students. She and her husband live in Atlanta now, and I don't want to give Emma the idea that the flame's still burning."

Chapter 2

To err is human. To really foul things up requires a computer.

— Anonymous

Cramer was in the office by 7:30 a.m. Monday, and already had a pot of coffee made and was on his second cup when his new secretary arrived. Michele Poe was an attractive woman, no doubt about it, but Cramer was not one of those executives who wanted just a pretty face at the front desk. He wanted competence, loyalty, and confidence, and he had gotten exactly that when he hired Michele. Judging by her recommendations, Michele's former employers were aware she wanted to find something closer to home, and had willingly but with obvious regret given her the highest recommendations. Furthermore, she suffused the whole office with the cheeriness of a field of daisies.

"It's going to be pretty slow around here for the first couple of days," Cramer said as he was packing his briefcase, "so if you've got any personal correspondence to catch up on, now's the time. About all that we need to do right now is to finish putting up the books and do whatever straightening up I didn't finish last week."

"This may be the easiest job I ever had," Michele said with a perky smile.

"Well, there is one other thing that should occupy you for a little while," Cramer noted. "Have you ever used this software before?" The accountant pointed to a stack of manuals at least 18 inches high.

Michele quickly examined them. "I know MS-DOS, of course," she said. "But the word processing program is different from the one we used at Peat. So is the spreadsheet program. And the Compaq is new to me."

"You probably had something a bit more powerful at Peat," Cramer said. "This will do everything we're going to need to do for a long time to come, though. Tell you what, plan to spend your time getting to be the most proficient operator in Atlanta on this setup. Then, when things start picking up, we'll be off to a running start. If you need me, I'll be at this number. Just ask for Will Posey, and he can track me down."

★   ★   ★

Based on the map, the trip to the Coca-Cola headquarters in downtown Atlanta from suburban Sandy Springs was a fairly direct one, using Roswell Road. Direct it was; quick it wasn't. Cramer got his first taste of the storied Atlanta traffic, a taste that threw him a quarter of an hour late. He noticed that Georgia Tech University was across the street from Coke. He didn't like being late, because Lenny Cramer was always on time, and his usually equable temperament was somewhat frayed when he finally arrived at Posey's office.

The Coke executive was an old friend of Cramer, but that didn't make him feel any better about being late. As a veteran of years in the Atlanta traffic trenches, Posey was understanding and a trifle amused at his friend's discomfort. He quickly restored Cramer's equanimity and took Cramer to an available office where they discussed the audit.

Since this project was an operational audit, there was no need for the CPA to follow many of the time-consuming steps a full audit would require. In a regular audit an accountant tests samples of inventory, receivables, and payables. The accountant will ask banks to confirm the amount of cash in the business's accounts and send form letters to outside companies that have contracts with the firm being audited. The purpose is to confirm that the other companies exist and that the various contracts or receivables are real.

Cramer was a forensic accountant—he specialized in uncovering fraud in ledgers of big and small companies. Cramer liked to quote from a piece in the *Wall Street Journal*: "Other accountants may look at the charts. But forensic accountants actually dig into the body." The increase in malpractice suits against the big accounting firms and the huge fraud cases in the late eighties— such as the ZZZZ Best company—had created a need for accountants specializing in detecting fraud.

13

One example which Cramer used in his auditing class was the notorious Equity Funding Fraud. Here nonexistent insurance policy records were added to the customer master file of the organization. This fiction was created by unscheduled file updating outside the mainstream of normal data processing operations. Then there was the example of Penn Central Railroad "misplacing" almost 400 railroad cars. The computerized system was modified so that the missing rail cars would not be noticed.

In fact, even as an operational audit it promised to be a relatively abbreviated engagement. Coke's divisional chief suspected one of his staff of improper practices. Thus, Cramer could confine his review, at least initially, to the activities of the suspect. He might have to give the appearance of a broader audit, just to avoid tipping off any inquisitive and particularly observant employees, but the inquiry would still target just one individual.

The suspect was Dan Mays. From all outward appearances, Mays was an unlikely candidate to be playing games with Coca-Cola's corporate checkbook. He had been with the division for 12 of the 19 years he had been with Coke, beginning as a computer operator. After attending night school and taking a junior college associate degree in business, he had worked himself up to the point where he was in charge of payroll for the international division and its 230 employees.

Cramer began by conferring with the supervisor of overseas development. The CPA explained that the division was looking at its computer requirements, and asked for a brief outline of the operations the supervisor needed the computer to do. He got more than he requested. For 45 minutes, he listened to a long and exquisitely detailed explanation of the needs for the overseas development crew, and a string of complaints about the low priority it had been assigned for computer access. Cramer finally managed to rid himself of the over-zealous executive, but not before he had been promised "a full, complete draft of our ongoing and vastly expanded needs within 48 hours." The CPA pledged to review the draft carefully, and gratefully ushered the visitor out the door.

The next two interviews went more swiftly, and by 11:30 Cramer was ready to talk to the payroll chief, who all along had been the only one he was really interested in. The other interviews had only been smoke screens that Cramer hoped would allay any suspicions the target of the audit might have. He wanted to get a first-hand look at Mays. Face-to-face conferences were not a required auditing tool, but Cramer had more than once learned that taking personal measure of an adversary could be productive. He wished he had a second person to help in the interview to listen and act as a witness.

"I guess Joe explained that we're taking a look at the division's computer requirements," Cramer said as he ushered Mays into the small office. "This discussion is just a quick run-through for me, to give me some on-the-ground grasp of what you're doing now, and what the divisional personnel think we should be doing, if anything. Obviously, we'll be going into a lot more depth later, and you'll be talking with other consultants in a lot more detail. I'm just a CPA with limited computer expertise, but we want to be sure what procedures you have in place so we'll know what changes are indicated, if any. How about giving me a quick run-down on how you handle your end of things."

Mays quickly launched into an explanation of the payroll process. It was all very general, Cramer noted, except that Mays did seem to dwell a trifle long on the accounting safeguards included in payroll production. On the other hand, the CPA reflected, perhaps I'm just being overly suspicious. Cramer wanted to maintain control by clearly establishing the facts and to counter future denials.

"Do you just handle payroll," Cramer finally asked, "or do you have other functions?"

"Well," Mays responded, "we have some accounts payable... minor stuff, like office supplies and such. I take care of those, but they're pretty small. Just stuff central purchasing doesn't normally carry. Maybe flowers when one of the employees has a loss in the family, and that sort of thing. We pay all of those on the basis of vouchers that both Joe and I have to sign."

Cramer knew that body language was important in any interview or interrogation. An innocent person will sit upright in the chair, maintain strong eye contact, and give quick answers and denials. They may become angry or hostile. Whereas a guilty person may be more passive, playing a cat and mouse game with false clues. Nontruthful answers may cause dry mouth and lips, that result in a clicking sound when speaking. A dishonest person may avoid eye contact or stare at the interviewer and then drop the eyes down or away as they answer a question. Restlessness and shifting in a chair, abnormal eye-blink rate, and biting of the lips or tongue are other tell-tale signs of dishonest answers. An auditor has to observe both verbal and nonverbal signals during the investigative process.

Cramer wrapped up the interview just before lunch, as he had planned. He'd wanted to listen to and take a measure of Mays, not answer any questions. Thus, the timing of the interview was part of

Cramer's plan. It gave Cramer the excuse to cut off discussion when he'd sized up the payroll clerk.

The CPA had made previous arrangements to meet Posey at the Diplomat, in downtown Atlanta. It was unlikely that anybody else from the division would be frequenting that restaurant, Posey had explained, and lunch would give the two time to review the morning's events.

"Looks like you're becoming a veteran of Atlanta traffic already," Posey grinned, sliding a Coke toward Cramer as he eased into a chair. "You're only seven minutes late."

"I am reminded of the injunction, 'All things come to him who waits,'" Cramer sighed. "I hope so, because it seems I'll be spending a large part of my life from now on waiting in mini-traffic jams."

"Don't worry about it. You may be late but you're impeccably dressed."

Cramer laughed. "What can I say, Will? The auditor's dress code is a dark, preferably pin-striped, suit. Let's face it, clients trust conservatively dressed auditors. Besides, I've noticed you business executives 'dress for success' the same way." Cramer paused to smile. "At least I *look* like I know what I'm doing." Both men grinned at Cramer's self-deprecation.

"How's it going in the office?" Posey queried. "Found any skunks in any woodpiles?"

"I haven't even begun looking for a woodpile yet," Cramer said. "I've talked to your man Mays, though, along with a couple of other chaps. He seems cool enough. Certainly is ready to convince you at the drop of a double-entry ledger that the payroll system is close to foolproof. And that's without even being asked."

"So what's next on the agenda?"

"Well, I've got one more interview set up for this afternoon. It isn't necessary, but I don't want to spook Mays. This way, I'm hoping he won't get the idea that I'm focusing on him. After that comes an examination of the payroll records, starting with Mays himself. If we're lucky, and if there is something going on, we'll find it right off. If not, then we'll expand the scope of things."

"Good. I told you about Jeanne Saxet. She's been with Joe ever since he joined Coca-Cola. I'd stake my reputation, such as it is, on her discretion, and so would Joe. In fact, considering his occasional philandering, he probably has. Joe has assigned Jeanne to you for whatever time you need her. She knows just about anything you should need to know about office routine, records-keeping, the whole nine yards. Plus she is thoroughly versed on our computer operation."

"Good," Cramer replied, just as the prime rib arrived. "I'll need her this afternoon, as soon as I finish with this final interview. That's when we'll start actually trying to determine what Mr. Mays has been up to. If anything."

★　　★　　★

Cramer had three possible ways to audit the computer records. First, he could use the vouching approach to audit around the computer. He could treat the computer as a "black box" and avoid any scrutiny of the computer system itself. He could follow the audit trail up to where computer processing began and then pick up the trail on the other side of processing by examining printouts. However, Statements on Auditing Standards (SAS) No. 3 specifies that an auditor must develop a knowledge of the computer and may not rely on computer specialists. Computer systems now often generate a huge quantity of data which are beyond the scope of ticking and checking the transaction documents. Auditing around the computer is acceptable only where certain conditions are met. Specifically, this approach is appropriate where justified on a cost/benefit basis as compared to other available techniques. This approach is never appropriate where its use is solely justified by the auditor's lack of EDP expertise.

Under the second approach—the verification method—an auditor develops independent means of verifying the existence, ownership, and valuation of assets. For example, in a regular audit, Cramer would use an inquiry program to obtain a sample printout of the computerized account files and then confirm these balances by circularizing the account holders.

Under the third option, the systems approach, the auditor appraises the control features of the computer system to determine if the objectives of the system have been met. If the computer controls are effective, then the auditor can generally assume that the data output is correct, assuming that the *input* data is correct.

Cramer decided to use the verification approach. He began by immediately zeroing in on the suspect, pulling up on the computer all of Mays' pay records for the past two years and comparing them with the actual paperwork. The CPA was looking for differences between computer entries and the paper trail left by the division's accounting system. If Mays was as astute as he had appeared in the interview, Cramer knew the rifle-shot approach would be a long shot, but it was worth a try. And, as things turned out, that's all it ended up being —

just a try. The computer entries tallied perfectly with the accompanying paperwork.

Cramer had been looking for one dodge in particular. It had seemed a likely chance after he had done some initial comparisons. All the data entered on the division's timekeeping and payroll system on the computer carried both the employee's name and his employee number. Manually, though, all processing and control was based on the employee's name alone, since the division was small and everyone was known to everyone else. The reverse was true for the computerized system, however. All the processing was done by numbers. The computer even used numbers, without any reference to employees' names, to look up names and addresses to print payroll checks.

Anyone with larcenous intent who had pondered that could have used it in several fashions to feather his nest, Cramer knew. He recalled one case in Harrisburg, Pennsylvania, where the payroll supervisor had filled out fake overtime forms for employees, but entered his own employee number in the computer.

Obviously, Mays had not been sticking his hand in the Coca-Cola till through that particular loophole. Cramer was back at square one.

Chapter 3

A member (CPA) shall be independent in the performance of professional services as required by standards promulgated by bodies designated by council (of the AICPA).

Rule 101

The crystal octagon continued its halting but unvarying revolutions. Ninety degrees, then a pause while a right index finger absently stroked the chilled dew from the sloping facet of the glass. About every revolution and a half, the glass rose, tilted a fraction of Pepsi across the waiting lips, then descended to resume the circling libational ballet that had begun almost an hour before. Although he would not tell his current employer, he, like Mike Tyson, liked arch- rival Pepsi better than Coke.

Lenny Cramer was in one of his famous abstracted moods, what Becc called his "terminal trances," oblivious to all around him. Not that there was that much to which to be oblivious. Becc had already gone to bed, and Cramer had never been much of one for background music or television. The house was quiet, with only the muted rumble of the Roswell Road traffic intruding on its silence. He was breaking his personal rule, never to drink caffeine after 9:00 in the evening. Three hours from now he would be wide awake. For some reason he remembered the fact that a bottle of soda contains approximately one-fourth the amount of caffeine as a cup of brewed coffee, and about one-third that of tea.

He was mulling over the day's events. The Coca-Cola audit was not going badly. By any measure, it was far too early to make that judgment. But Cramer did want to wrap it up with a minimum of expense to his client. He wanted the company's divisional superintendent as a reference later, and the quicker he could get to the bottom of matters at the soft-drink company, the greater the likelihood of a glowing reference. That meant either he needed a lot of luck in identifying any misuse or misappropriation of funds, or he needed to zero in on the process that was being misused. Lenny Cramer had never been one to trust anything to luck. That left only one other alternative—raw intelligence. Thus the deep contemplation.

Two' possible scams he had already eliminated in the past hour. One was the salami technique.

Though not particularly sophisticated, this technique had proved effective many times for the larcenously inclined, Cramer knew. Someone with appropriate access randomly reduces accounts by a tiny fraction of what each totals, normally 10 to 15 cents, and reallocates the funds to another account within the system. The money is then drawn down. Because the funds are simply rearranged within the system, no controls are breached. The losses to each account are so minimal they either go unnoticed or unreported. Such scams work moderately well with large numbers of accounts held by many people, as in the banking system. They also could work internally with one corporation, if inventories were the salami being sliced, rather than funds. In the case of Coke's international division, though, Cramer knew that the number of accounts was insufficient to generate any substantial amount of cash, even if someone was using the salami technique. The same was true of inventory salami-slicing. About all a thief could get would be enough Cokes to supply a middle-sized fourth of July party.

The other technique he was confident could be eliminated was the round-down. Such schemes required great numbers of accounts that involved percentage chargeables or payables, such as credit cards or savings accounts. Frequently, when a sum is multiplied by the required percentage, the result is less than a full cent. In round-downs, the swindler randomly chooses a number of the accounts to round down to the nearest cent. The fraction of a cent then goes into a separate account to which he has access. The customer loses nothing, since he would not have received the fraction of a cent anyway, and he is never the wiser. With large numbers of accounts, the technique can add up to large sums being misappropriated. But, just as in the salami technique, Coke simply did not have the volume of accounts required for such a scam to work.

"No, the fraudulent technique had to be something else, something quite simple and direct, probably some weekly or monthly expense incurred by the division that would be obvious once spotted," thought

Cramer. "Possibly it is one that would surface in a full-scale audit, but I have to find it a lot quicker than that."

The glass paused midway in one of its upward swings, then slowly drifted downward again. The revolutions stopped, then resumed again abruptly for a 180-degree turn before the glass swiftly made a full trip back up. Cramer, the faraway look vanished, swished down the last of the Pepsi, then strode to the sink and dumped the ice. With a smile of obvious satisfaction, he flipped off the light on the way to his bedroom for what he wished would be a night of sound sleep.

★   ★   ★

Posey was right. Jeanne Saxet knew her business—and just about everybody else's, too.

"Jeanne, do all the employees of the international division work here in Atlanta?" Cramer asked as soon as he was settled into his temporary office the next morning.

"Oh, no," the secretary quickly replied. "We have quite a few who work elsewhere. "There are several in New York, for example, who work out of the offices of another Coke division there, though we have jurisdiction over them. There is a small branch in Los Angeles that takes care of much of the Asian market. And, of course, at any given time we'll have operatives in several foreign locations, establishing new markets. Those are permanently assigned to this office, though they may stay out-of-country for as much as a year or two."

"The New York and L.A. staff...they're permanently assigned there?" Cramer asked. "How are they paid?"

"By bank transfer, I think, in every case," Jeanne said.

"How about expenses? Do they have expense accounts? If they do, how are they paid?"

"Now that you ask, I'm not sure how they're paid," the secretary replied thoughtfully. "I know they each send in an accounting each month. I've seen those. But I'm not sure exactly how payment is handled."

"Tell you what, Jeanne, please pull me a hard copy of the New York and L.A. staff roster. Then let's take a look at their last few expense accounts," Cramer said. It was difficult to keep the edge of excitement from his voice.

Within 15 minutes, the auditor's suspicions had been confirmed. As noon approached, he called Posey and suggested they have lunch together.

"It was simple, once I thought about it," Cramer told the Coke executive as they nibbled at their salads. "It all tied back to your accounting system. Payables to the staff..uh salary and expenses...are all processed by name, though the employee number appears on the forms. But for the computer bookkeeping, it's all done by number. So, Mays has been submitting phony expense forms for the staffers in New York and Los Angeles. When it goes on the computer, though, he inserts his employee number. The funds have been deposited directly into a separate bank account he established.

"Since employees don't get W2 forms or a Form 1099 for out-of-pocket expenses they are reimbursed, they were never aware of the scam. He was issuing two checks, one to the employee for the legitimate expenses and one to him that was direct-deposited. Mays is randomly rotating the bogus expense checks among the various out-of-town staffers. Not too sophisticated, but effective for a time."

"Good job, Lenny," Posey said enthusiastically. "I knew we'd gotten the right man. Any idea how much he's gotten away with?"

"Not yet, but you're not going to be looking at any losses that will shake Coca-Cola to it's fiscal foundations," Cramer replied. "This scheme is really pretty penny-ante stuff. The most I've found so far, going back about three months, is six or seven hundred dollars a month. It really depends on how long it's been going on. That isn't really the question, though."

"No?" Posey asked, puzzled. "What else is there?"

"Well," Cramer went on, choosing his word carefully. "You can cure this problem pretty easily, just by getting rid of Mays. And you can probably prevent a recurrence of this particular scam by changing your accounting procedures slightly. One way to do that, for example, is for all computer accounting procedures to append to each employee's number the first three letters of his surname. That way it's readily apparent to anyone who's looking, that something is awry. What bothers me is that we've caught a greedy little guppy, but you may be letting sharks into the swimming pool."

"What do you mean?" Posey asked.

"Well ... Will, I hope you know me well enough to know that I'm not going to start crying 'Wolf' just to generate a little business. But your computer security is awfully loose. There have been a couple of times in the past few days that I've been astonished at the virtually unrestricted access that Jeanne has, for example...don't get me wrong.

I'm not saying Jeanne has done anything wrong, or has even thought about it, for that matter. She seems to be the epitome of the dedicated, loyal, and totally honest employee. But with all the data locked up in your computer, access should be tightly controlled. It should be almost like military secrets, on a 'need-to-know' basis."

"So what do you suggest?" Posey asked.

"I think you need to have someone with more expertise than me take a look at what you're doing, and see where things need to be tightened up. I'm not trying to expand the scope of what you hired me to do just to keep drawing my consultation fee. Believe me, there's a lot of potential for some major harm."

"Certainly I believe you," Posey said with a grin. "I've never doubted you ever since that time you told me you could talk that damned parakeet of mine down out of a tree after he escaped—and you did it."

"I never did tell you about the bird seed I had in the rim of my hat, did I?" Cramer chuckled.

"No, you didn't," Posey said, loosing an explosive laugh. "And for years I've been telling that story, about my friend with the mystical way with animals. You're nothing but a lousy con man yourself. Now tell me: What're you on to here? What exactly do you want us to do? Remember, that's not our computer. It belongs to Uncle Jemima...who, now that I think about it...is on vacation for a couple of weeks."

"I took the liberty of making a call this morning to Howard Nelson. You remember Howie, the kid from Texas who received his undergraduate degree from Baylor. Well, Howie is on the faculty at Wharton now. As soon as he earned enough at poker to pay his way through his last year of the MBA program he straightened up and turned into a first-class student, all the way through a Ph.D. He's a bit of a specialist in computer auditing principles. Howie said he's got a grad student who has already earned his CPA, and has taken off a semester before he starts on his dissertation which focuses on expert systems. He's right here in Atlanta. Howie said if anyone can find which buttons are available to be pushed by the wrong people, it's this fellow. His name's Beauregard Duncan. They call him 'Bo.' In fact, he may be the only man I know of who has two nicknames. They also call him 'Slam' Duncan, though why I don't know. Anyway, I thought you might be interested in talking to him, and having him take a look at the security controls you have. It may save you some major headaches down the road."

"I certainly like the idea," Posey said thoughtfully. "Of course, we'll have to take it up with Joe. Meanwhile, these steaks deserve something better than to be ignored."

Chapter 4

The practical objectives of all audits of financial
statements are to obtain and evaluate evidence about
these five assertions made by management in financial
statements: existence or occurrence, completeness, rights
and obligations, valuation or allocation, and presentation
and disclosure.

— Jack C. Robertson
Frederick G. Davis

"So ... what does it boil down to? On how long a ride have we been taken?" Joe Fred Lanniham impaled Cramer and Posey with one of his patented piercing gazes.

"I don't think I've ever known anyone who could simultaneously look determined and sound resigned," Cramer mused. "Of course, I don't guess I've known too many guys who've been in his shoes, either, looking at their career spiraling down the toilet because they couldn't stay faithful to a lifelong marital commitment. Even a non-religious person should know there's an ultimate price to pay for immorality."

"Not nearly as bad as it could be, Joe," Posey responded. "It looks like Mays has been massaging the expense reports of the people in the New York and L.A. offices for about two and a half years now, submitting fake expense reports and having the payments deposited into an account at a Citizens and Southern branch in Fairburn. Best Lenny can make out, he's snared about $19,000."

"Is he nailed?" Lanniham demanded. Posey turned to Cramer.

"Oh, yes, I don't think there's any question about that," Cramer interposed. "We've got the account number at Fairburn C&S, where he's been making the deposits. Shouldn't be difficult at all to establish whose account it is, even if he's been using an assumed name. He's also left a wide paper trail. Some of the expense reports are obvious forgeries, once you start looking for them. I don't think there's going to be much difficulty at all in getting a conviction."

"Conviction?" Lanniham's voice rose a quarter-register. "Uh, well, uh, yes, that's one of the alternatives we'll have to examine, of course. Considering the nature of the case, though, we'll also have to take a look at whether it's in the company's best interest to pursue a criminal action. You know...there are a couple of considerations: the lost time from work that the witnesses would have, and the bad publicity when an employee is publicly identified as a thief. Maybe it's best just to get rid of Mays and write off the loss. Besides, we don't want to give anybody else any ideas, now, do we?"

Cramer and Posey glanced furtively at each other. "Yes, Will," Cramer thought, "I'm reading this hand just like you. If Lanniham tries to ship Mays off to jail, the wife is going to raise cane, and one of the first things that she's going to raise cane about is the little fling she had with the boss. That'll cost Lanniham not only his job, but his wife. He's in a sticky wicket. On the other hand, if he just lets the guy know what he has, he can force him to resign, get the wife transferred to another division, and let the ex-girlfriend know that if their previous cozy relationship ever surfaces, her husband is headed downriver to be tailored for a striped suit. He can do it under the guise of avoiding some bad press for the company. Nice finesse."

"Oh, I agree, Joe," Posey said. "One thing we don't want bandied around is that it's easy to embezzle Coke's hard-earned money. Along those lines, Lenny had some interesting observations the other day. He seems to think that maybe we ought to take a closer look at all our computer security. Appears that it's not at all difficult for people to get sticky fingers, as lax as the Syrup Set has been in handling the computer processing."

"You dangle the bait so enticingly," Cramer thought, "letting Lanniham know that maybe his old foe Uncle Jemima has a chink in his corporate armor."

"How does that affect us?" Lanniham asked. "That's Clifford's department. If he's got a problem, then we need to let him know about it."

"It was almost like taking a dose of castor oil for him to say that," Cramer thought. "These two *really* don't like each other. So let's see how far he's willing to go with this game of corporate one-upmanship."

"We don't know that there are any problems, Joe. Or at least any problems that have resulted in any other losses. What Lenny tells me, though, is that the whole system lacks any kind of meaningful security. If that's the case, then it is our business. We've got data on that system that can't be replaced. *And* data that we don't want to fall into the wrong hands. Lenny tells me he can get someone in for a few weeks, let him take a look at the access we have to the system, and determine if it's too unrestricted. There'd be almost no contact with the other division. They wouldn't even have to know we're doing it. I know it would be best to wait till Uncle Jemima ... uh, Clifford ... is back from his vacation, but Lenny tells me this fellow is the best, and he's only going to be available for a few weeks. He's out of Philadelphia, and as I understand it, he is here to see his folks. If anything comes of it, we'll kick it over to Clifford immediately."

"You are smooth, Will, you silver-tongued rascal," Cramer thought admiringly. "I never knew you had it in you to play these games so skillfully. He's here to see his folks, all right—for four months. Without ever saying so, you've let Lanniham know he can turn this debacle with Mays into a star in his crown, if he can uncover some real serious security problems in the other division. At the same time, if things are as loose over there as they seem to be with the computer system, Lanniham can slap it to a corporate rival like a spoiled mackerel right in the face. And he can have it all in place before Clifford ever gets back into town and gets wind of anything. Neat, real neat."

Cramer watched with amusement as Lanniham almost visibly went through the same mental scenario. Finally, the division chief unfolded his hands and stood up.

"Okay, Will, whatever you think is best. Just don't get in anybody's hair over there on the Syrup side, and for goodness sake don't give anybody the idea we think they're running a sloppy operation. Any accessing you do, I want it to be confined as far as possible to those programs we're supposed to be screwing around with, not the Syrup Set's database. And Lenny, I don't want anybody planning to buy their vacation cottage with Coca-Cola auditing fees. Keep the time down, and keep the fees reasonable. I've got to get to a meeting downtown at the Trust Company, but I want to hear from you in a couple of days."

Turning to Will, Lanniham said, "Get Mays out of the office till 4 o'clock today. Send him on whatever errands you can find, and have Jeanne cut his final paycheck. Give him his accrued vacation, but no severance pay. We'll wrap up any loose ends later, but at 4 o'clock I want him and you in my office so I can personally fire him. Run me a copy of several of those forged expense accounts, too. Just to make sure we got it cinched down, call one of the people in L.A. and one in New York on the latest expense accounts. Tell 'em there's been some kind of screw-up here. Go over their original submission, and verify that the bogus expenses were never incurred. Remember: 4 o'clock, with his final paycheck ready. That scheming scumbag."

"One other thing. Check the job board. See what job is available in Connie Mays' pay bracket for which she qualifies. I sure don't want a disgruntled wife making waves in my division."

As Cramer left the office, he noticed a brightly colored book on Lanniham's desk. It was entitled *Coca-Cola Superstar*, by Fiora S. Palazzini.

★   ★   ★

"May I speak to Mr. Duncan, please?" Cramer asked.

"Sure. Take your choice," the voice replied, too jauntily for Cramer's taste. "You want a Mr. Duncan who's drawing Social Security, a Mr. Duncan who right now is drawing a beer—that's me—or a Mr. Duncan who's drawing flies while he's trying to get a tan in the back yard? That's my little brother, bless his pea-pickin' soul and curse his pluperfect pectorals."

"Uh, Mr. Beauregard Duncan. From Wharton."

"You got him. What can I do for you?"

"This is Lenny Cramer. I'm a CPA. I was on the faculty at Wharton until recently. Dr. Nelson suggested I get in touch with you about an audit I'm involved in here in Atlanta."

"Howie! How's he doing? Did he ever get his office straightened out after setting fire to the wastebasket with his pipe? Funniest thing I've seen since a cat dropped a litter in Mrs. Calliham's basket of clean laundry, right on top of her stack of step-ins."

"Yes, he's got everything back into shape again. Not much damage, except to the wastebasket and a few books." Cramer, normally not one to make snap judgements, made an exception in this case. He decided he liked neither this impudent young man nor the prospect of working with him. He was on the verge of terminating the conversation when two thoughts, tumbling over each other for acknowledgment, stopped him. First was memory of Howie Nelson's ringing recommendation of Duncan. "The absolute best at wringing dirty laundry out of a computer," Nelson had said. The second was the recollection that Lanniham had placed him on a short lease, time-wise. The likelihood of finding

28

anybody truly qualified in so short of time was slim, especially considering the nature of the job.

"Look, Mr. Duncan, I know ..."

"Call me Slam, please," Duncan interrupted. "My folks didn't have any boy-children they gave the first name of 'Mr.' to."

"I know this is short notice," Cramer continued, unable to bring himself to be so familiar as to use a nickname. "But I wonder if you could possibly drop by my office in Sandy Springs this evening about 5:30? I'd like to talk to you about the audit I'm on. It shouldn't take but half an hour or so, and I'll be happy to pay your regular consultation fee."

"Sure. Just give me the address. I'm just a little south of the loop so it won't take me long at all."

★　　　★　　　★

Cramer was just opening the door to the office when he was startled by a motorcycle careening into the driveway. Cramer did *not* ride motorcycles. He did not *like* motorcycles, viewing them with the same distaste that he had for hot rods, dune buggies, and the many other diverse manifestations of the inexplicable compulsion some people have to turn perfectly reasonable vehicles of transport into weird, uncomfortable, unsightly and frequently noisy contraptions. He instantly disliked this motorcycle more than most, since it sported an extended fork that tilted the bike so much it seemed someone had tried to turn the motorcycle into a mobile isosceles triangle. The rider astride the motorcycle seemed to have legs even longer than the fork that stretched interminably in front of the handlebars. He virtually undulated off the motorcycle and removed his helmet, revealing a shock of straight black hair as thick as a brand-new mop.

"Lenny Cramer? I'm Slam Duncan." The hand that engulfed Cramer's felt like it was broad enough to pick up a 55-gallon drum. The owner of the hand appeared to be approximately as tall as a moderate-sized New England lighthouse.

"Yes, I'm Dr. Cramer, of course. Glad to meet you." Cramer mentally kicked himself as he extracted his hand from the wrap-around grip. He never used the "Dr." People who insisted on announcing their academic credentials right off irritated him. But so did this six-foot-six apparition in front of him, and even without realizing it he wanted to put some distance between himself and Duncan. "Come on in. I told

29

my secretary to make a pot of coffee before she left. Let's see if she did."

"I'll pass on the coffee, thanks. Never drink anything that looks like it's made of floorsweep, I say. But you go ahead."

"I will, thank you. Why don't you grab a chair, and I'll be right with you." Cramer thought grimly, "I am not going to be a very happy camper for the next few days." With resignation, he put aside his distaste, and began briefing Duncan on the situation, leaving out any details on the office in-fighting and any references to Lanniham's indiscretions. Duncan sat quietly, listening intently as he unconsciously pulled at a forelock of long black hair. Cramer was surprised, when he got to the scam Mays had been pulling, at how quickly Duncan caught on. In fact, he had interrupted to ask if the expense accounts had been checked even before Cramer got around to telling him exactly what the scam had been. Then he had virtually barraged Cramer with questions about the division's computer security, methods of access, and so on, till finally the CPA had to call a halt. He was astonished to discover, on checking his watch, that almost three hours had passed.

This giant may be an odd duck, but he's no quack. He felt a bit more comfortable as he watched the lanky rider roar off, now officially associated in the operational audit.

★   ★   ★

That evening at home Cramer found his auditing lecture notes. He would be teaching a basic auditing course at Georgia State in the fall and he wanted to use E&Y's audit report of Coca-Cola as a handout. E&Y, of course, had issued the standard three-paragraph unqualified opinion. In 1988, the unqualified opinion report had been revised to include new wording and three paragraphs. An *unqualified* opinion gives a company a clean bill of health, but the accounting profession takes the position that a search for *defalcations* in financial statements requires audit procedures far beyond those normally used in a financial statement audit.

Cramer knew that conditions may prevent an auditor from following generally accepted auditing standards or the auditors might find something during the audit to stop them from reporting that the financial statements are fair in accordance with generally accepted accounting principles (GAAP). Thus, three other types of reports may be issued: a qualified opinion, a disclaimer, or an adverse opinion.

Two reasons may cause an auditor to issue a *qualified* opinion. First, something may prevent an auditor from performing all of the necessary audit procedures (e.g. the auditor being unable to examine records of a foreign subsidiary or to observe the inventory count). This is referred to as a scope limitation. Second, the auditor may decide that the company did not follow GAAP (e.g. the company improperly computing the value of inventory).

When financial statements are not presented fairly in accordance with GAAP, an auditor will issue an adverse or qualified opinion. Whether to use a qualified or adverse opinion depends on the extent to which the departure from GAAP affects the overall financial statements. An adverse opinion is rare. On the other hand, when an auditor lacks the knowledge to form any opinion on the financial statements, a disclaimer opinion is appropriate. This type of opinion may be used when the auditor lacks sufficient evidence to form an opinion.

Cramer read through the audit opinion.

Board of Directors and Shareholders
The Coca-Cola Company
Atlanta, Georgia

We have audited the accompanying balance sheets of Coca-Cola Company and its subsidiaries as of December 31, 1991 and 1990, and the related statements of income, retained earnings, and cash flows for the years then ended. These financial statements are the responsibility of the company's management. Our responsibility is to express an opinion on these financial statements based on our audits.

We conducted our audits in accordance with generally accepted auditing standards. Those standards require that we plan and perform the audit to obtain reasonable assurance about whether the financial statements are free of material misstatement. An audit includes examining, on a test basis, evidence supporting the amounts and disclosures in the financial statements. An audit also includes assessing the accounting principles used and significant estimates made by management, as well as evaluating the overall financial statement presentation. We believe that our audits provide a reasonable basis for our opinion.

In our opinion, the financial statements referred to above present fairly, in all material respects, the financial position of Coca-Cola Company and its subsidiaries at December 31, 1991 and 1990, and the results of its operations and its cash flows for the years then ended in conformity with generally accepted accounting principles.

Ernst & Young
February 1, 1992

He made a note to have copies made of the audit report for his students.

Chapter 5

Working papers should support an auditor's conclusions and, in an effort to promote understanding and minimize preparation time, should be clear, concise, and above all unambiguous. The sheer volume of working paper generated during an audit engagement is inconsequential; quantity is no substitute for quality.

— David N. Ricchiute

Cramer had made arrangements to meet Duncan at the Coca-Cola offices at 10 o'clock the next morning. After a late start getting Becc off to school, he dropped into his own office to see how things were going, and to pick up his briefcase. There he found Michele, immersed in the intricacies of learning the new computer system. She seemed to have things well in hand. There had been no telephone calls. The world of corporate Atlanta was taking its time in beating a path to his door, as he had resigned himself to expect.

Cramer was always amused when he drove into the Coke complex. There was a gate with a guard. No one could enter the premises without a name tag. In order for someone to visit, the guard had to call someone inside who gave permission for the person to enter. Lenny parked in the visitor's parking lot and went into the building. His red name tag rested prominently on his coat lapel. He stopped at a Coke machine on the ground floor and got a free diet Coke from the machine. Was it taxable? Oh, well, the Internal Revenue Service was *probably* not that picky.

In this area were various displays of Coca-Cola memorabilia, promotional advertisements, and other promotional merchandise. There was a Russell Yo-Yo made in the Philippines, evolution of the Coke can, 1929 cold-box, chronology of bottles used between 1900 and 1956, an 1891 Coca-Cola calendar, a syrup urn used as a premium in the 1890s, and more. The displays reminded him of a family vacation trip he had made long ago as a kid.

During one summer vacation, Cramer's family traveled to Vicksburg, Mississippi, to see its historical attractions, including the Biedenharn Candy Company and Museum of Coca Cola Memorabilia. The museum was located in downtown Vicksburg on Washington Street. The restored building was where Coca Cola was first bottled in 1894. The museum also featured Coca Cola memorabilia, a 1900 soda fountain, and an 1890 candy store. One of his best memories of the museum, however, was not an historical artifact, but the delicious ice cream float and homemade candy that provided immense refreshment on a hot Mississippi summer day.

Cramer's parents both enjoyed historical attractions. His father was particularly fond of old battlefields. The Vicksburg National Military Park was renowned as one of the best. The 16 mile driving tour of the old battlefield was etched in his mind, even after all the intervening years. He remembered reading how two Missouri units, one Confederate and one Union, directly opposed one another at a strategic location. In bloody battle, friend met friend, brother met brother, and neighbor met neighbor.

Later that morning, at precisely 10 o'clock, Cramer was closeted with Posey and Duncan. Posey covered essentially the same ground Cramer had covered the night before, but not before exchanging a questioning glance at his old friend. Cramer simply shrugged slightly and raised his eyebrows a tad to show his own perplexity. After all, how do you explain a certified public accountant and alleged expert computer auditor who shows up for work toting a motorcycle helmet with a ninja warrior emblazoned across the back and wearing a Hawaiian flowered shirt that seemed to scream its colors. When Posey turned Cramer and Duncan over to his assistant, Laura Lee Bertone, Cramer could almost see the same thoughts bumping against each other in Posey's mind. They were no more numerous than his own.

"Tell me about your computer system. With so many subsidiaries in so many countries, how do you get the financial information to corporate headquarters?" Duncan asked abruptly.

"We don't compile the data at remote locations and send it by mail like some companies," Laura responded.

"I assume you are talking about Pepsi."

"Sh-h-h-h," whispered Laura, with her index finger at her mouth. "Don't mention the P-word in here." She laughed.

"Actually some time ago we replaced the time-sharing, mainframe processing with personal computers at each location, with an international data network."

"What about different accounting practices in the different countries?" Duncan asked.

"First we developed an integrated chart of accounts that defines our reporting needs. The chart has four sections: profit and loss, balance sheet, statistical accounts, and accounts for restatement or reclassification of the balance sheet and income statement account. Each remote location has a common framework under which to operate."

"Each location operates on inexpensive, compatible desktop PCs. The local accounting personnel enter the data into the PC. The local accountant is more familiar with its content." Laura paused.

"The local person translates their local currency data, such as pounds, into U.S. dollars..."

"According to SFAS Nos. 52 and 8, of course," Duncan interrupted.

"Of course! They report this data in both local currency and U.S. dollars, in similar format to be reviewed by headquarters' personnel. They—the local office—lock the data so that it can not be changed at a future date and send it over a telecommunication network to headquarters. The main office can pull each location's financial information into its PC network."

"What security procedures do you employ?" Duncan asked.

"Hopefully a good, safe system. We have designated microcomputer rooms, security stations with steel door, passwords..."

"Passwords are notoriously ineffective as an access-control technique," Duncan almost shouted.

"We have a user identity code and automatic password obsolescence on a short-time cycle basis. Further, to use the computer the valid user must be at a valid terminal on a valid day of the week. To stop an illegal person from accessing the computer while the legal person is also using the system, the computer checks and will disconnect both users. We believe that securing the mainframe is not enough. More computer processing power is in the PCs on our employees' desks than at the data center."

"Do you have TEMPESTs on your PCs?"

"Not yet. You are referring to the prevention of our PCs from radiating electromagnetic signals.

We don't have any sensitive, classified governmental information in our system. The COKE formula is locked in a bank vault at Trust Company of Georgia."

"How about cryptographic technology to protect your communication signals?"

"No. Again, we are not NASA."

"What about separation of duties?"

"Data input and data output analysis are performed by different people. Library file procedures, programming, and actual system use are done by different people. We try to stop the fraud from occurring, but if fraud does occur, we can probably detect it."

"Hey," Cramer realized as Duncan put a particularly pointed question to Laura, "this guy knows what he's talking about. At least Howie wasn't wrong about his technical expertise. I wonder if he's ever seen that ridiculous motorcycle, though."

Laura continued her discussion for about fifteen more minutes, and then Duncan was left to check the audit trail within the computer system. Duncan knew that a good audit trail was an essential control feature in a computer system. He checked the logs of the unsuccessful sign-on attempts and the unsuccessful access attempts. Duncan did not finish his review of the security controls until 7:10 that evening.

He made a note to check with Laura about Coke's contingency plans for a fire in the data processing center. Were most of the computer software stored in off-site fireproof safes? He knew that three out of four businesses hit by fire could not survive the 90 days necessary to rebuild a destroyed computer system. He had read of the fire that destroyed Worlco, Inc. in 1984, a $25 million insurance and health care business. Due to planning, this company was able to resume collection and payments clerically and by a computer in a service bureau in a nearby city. What if a bursting pipe flooded the computer center? Suppose a disgruntled employee reformatted the hard disks?

"So ... how about we talk about this over lunch?"

Laura Lee Bertone brushed back a lock of dark red hair and glanced up from the terminal. Duncan, whom she had worked with briefly during the past two days, was looming over her right elbow, holding a sheaf of papers.

"What's that?" she asked.

"The standardized immatrization synchronization for the primary syncolathe during the past quarter," Duncan replied.

"What?" Bertone reached for the papers and quickly rifled through them. "What is this? A laundry bill. A book report. A magazine. This is a ... what did you call it?"

"The quarterly standardized immatrization synchronization for the primary syncolathe, or something like that. But you can call it anything you wish. Call it an old laundry bill. Call it a dog-eared copy of *Field & Stream*. What I'd rather do is call it an invitation to lunch. How about it?"

"Uh...sounds fine. Give me a minute to write this onto the disk and pop by the ladies' room. Just one question: do we have to discuss how you starch your shirts? Or can we confine it to the flies to use when you're looking for rainbows?"

"We can talk about whatever you wish, dear lady, though I'd prefer to spend my time talking only about you."

"Short conversation. Be back in a second."

★   ★   ★

"You're kidding. You jest. You can't be serious. That's what we're going to lunch on?" Bertone looked at the motorcycle with dismay.

"Sure," Duncan replied.

You really expect me to go to lunch on something out of a motorcycle gang flick? I can't do that."

"Sure you can. You're wearing slacks. I brought an extra helmet today, just for you. You'll like it. Naturally air-conditioned. Specially designed to make you feel you're a part of your environment. The ambiance of transportation at its absolute best."

"You're impossible, Slam," Bertone laughed. "Okay, but get out of here quick, will you, before somebody sees me? Please, don't try any loops or rolls, and take it slow. I value every single part of my anatomy just like it is. I don't want anything rearranged by somebody's bumper."

"A sentiment about your anatomy that I share completely," Slam said as he buckled on her helmet.

"The Varsity," Bertone said. "Now that's a switch for a luncheon date. I haven't been here in ages, since I dated a Georgia Tech student years ago."

"We could try someplace else," Duncan said, though not with much enthusiasm.

"Oh, no, it's perfect," Bertone responded quickly. "Nothing would go better with a Harley than a Varsity hot dog. We will eat inside, though. I'm putting my foot down on that. Besides, there's no place to hang a tray on this contraption."

"Whatever you say, m'lady. It does seem to me, though, that if you're going to be dining at the world's largest drive-in, you ought to be willing to experience it fully."

"I'm going to experience it fully from inside. And, I suspect my co-workers will experience a bit of it, too, when I get back to the office, because I'm going to get a double-dose of onions on my hot dog."

"Tell me about yourself," Duncan said after they'd received their hot dogs and fries and soft drinks. "Are you from here? Where did you go to school? How long have you been with Coke? Do you dye your eyes, or are they that color naturally? Can we do this tomorrow? Can we do it the day after tomorrow? When can I get you to pose for someone to paint your picture on your helmet?"

"Whoa, easy rider. One at a time, please. Yes, I'm from around here, sort of. I grew up in Savannah. My Dad died during my senior year in high school there. Mom managed to hang on until I graduated, but then we moved up here so I could go to school at Georgia State and she could go to work in my uncle's business. He runs an auto parts store in Smyrna, and Mom was his office manager until she died several years ago."

"So you're a Georgia State alumna," Duncan commented.

"I went full-time for two and a half years. Then I had to go to work for a small CPA firm after Mom's death. Worked in accounting for three years and finished my degree at night school. Then I left the public accounting firm and came to Coke where I've been the last four years.

"Why did you stop the public accounting work?"

"I don't have time to tell you about the thousands of tax returns I completed. Auditing was more interesting, but what I really liked was programming and doing other work on the computer. I had an opportunity to work more in the computer area here at Coke. Besides I was just plain tired of public accounting. Who knows why?"

Laura paused for a moment and then looked into Slam's eyes. "The eyes are my own, all the way. And I don't know about tomorrow, or the day after, or next year. But if we do do this again, I'll tell you right now we won't be moseying out on that piece of motorized mayhem out there. I don't exactly trust the driving skills of a guy whose jacket features a ninja warrior on the back. Meanwhile, we'd better finish these up and get back to the office. I want to be off that motorcycle before the rest of the crew starts returning from what I suspect was a far saner lunch hour than I had."

Her smile, Duncan decided, showed she didn't mean a word of it.

Later that night Duncan thought about Laura. She had those eyes that were so hard to explain, like intangible assets. They were special but not because they were so beautifully blue. They had those sparkles that tell *you* that she has a special interest in you. Yes, they were beautiful, but Laura's eyes were more. Her piercing gaze revealed a sharp mind working behind those eyes. She was attractive and intelligent, resourceful and independent. She was competing in a man's world which had been slow in opening its managerial doors and executive suites to women. Duncan felt a suspicion growing that he was in for some novel learning experiences with Laura—assuming that she was interested in him at all. Duncan realized he was scowling at himself, and wondered why.

Chapter 6

To protect against computer crimes, accountants should be *accountants*. There is no substitute for the old accounting nose, for the old investigative nose. You just have to do your homework.

— August Bequai

"Maybe I'm not supposed to ask this, but I'm going to anyway." The words were spoken lightly, as Laura tilted her head slightly to the left. The mannerism was one of the first things Slam had noticed about her. Never to the right, and never more than a little off the vertical. He found it charming.

"Ask, m'lady," Slam replied. "Can I make ice cream sodas the old fashioned way, sodas that would lure a leopard out of a tree? Do I sleep in socks? Does baldness run in my family? Are fatigues really my favorite apparel? Are most Mensa members egocentric insecure bores? Is there life after 30? Do I want to take you on a romantic cruise to the South Seas and live on coconuts and palm wine while the Polynesian breezes play harmony for the melodies my heart sings always when I am near you? The answer is yes, and yes, and yes again."

"The answer, m'lord, to all of the foregoing questions is that you can be the most exasperatingly irreverent ball of blarney I've ever encountered."

"Ah ... You've found my one weakness. Flattery. Give me more."

"What are you and Dr. Cramer doing at the office? I know it's something out of the ordinary. You're in the office all day long, and it's been a couple of weeks now. What's going on? Has somebody been embezzling money, or something like that? Everybody in the office is curious. First Dan Mays submits his resignation without any notice. And now his wife's been transferred over to another division."

"It's the Grinch," Slam replied.

"The what?"

"The Grinch," Slam repeated. "The Grinch that stole Christmas. He's stashed it in a Coca-Cola warehouse somewhere, and we're trying to smoke it out. So far, all we've turned up is a couple of missing Easters and one lost Ground Hog Day. But we're getting close. Just yesterday Cramer caught the scent of eggnog emanating out of a warehouse in Spokane. Turned out to be a conventioneer from Waco, Texas, though, who'd gone out there last New Year's and had such a good time he didn't make it back home on time. Now he's afraid to go home; his wife, it seems, is a butcher. Wields a mean cleaver."

"Be serious, Slam."

"Okay. Look, all we're doing is taking a look to see how secure the computer system is. It's no big thing. Somebody should have done it long ago."

"How secure? How secure does it need to be? My gosh, Coca-Cola isn't the Defense Department, even though we may like to think we're more important than the government. Somebody is going to steal classified Coca-Cola information, like how many days vacation a Clerk III has accrued? That's ridiculous."

"Not really," Slam responded. The jocularity was gone. "Every record on that computer represents time, if nothing else. Lose them, through negligence or malice, and it would cost Coke a pretty sum to compile them again. And that's assuming all of them could be reconstituted. Some of that data is stored only in the computer."

"You're right, I'm sure," Laura said. "I just got the impression it was more than that, that perhaps something was wrong."

"I think your job's safe," Slam said teasingly. "That is, unless you've got a garage full of purloined Christmas presents. Is that a strand of tinsel I detect deep in your auburn tresses?"

"That, I'm sure, is one of the many strands of gray hair I have acquired since I began spending too much time with a harebrained immigrant from some unknown planet," Laura replied, laughing. "The rink is right ahead. I'm going to warn you again. Pull any funny stuff out on the floor, and I'll cut you off at the knees. Roller-skating is not the best idea you've had. I prefer my wheels to come with an automatic transmission and velour seats."

"You have indeed shown admirable taste in that department," Slam said as he patted the Audi's upholstery. "But I still think we should have come on Themostoceles."

"No way, Jose," Laura said firmly. "If I have to take a trip to the hospital emergency room, I'm *not* going to do it on the back of a motorcycle. That's final."

★　　★　　★

Will Posey looked downcast, like a kid who'd just found out his favorite Saturday morning cartoon had been canceled. He looked at Cramer almost as if he was pleading.

"Are you sure? Don Ball is one of our best people. He's been our division employee of the month twice. He's never taken a single sick day. We have to force him to take vacations. He goes to my church. Heck, my daughter's even gone out with him a couple of times when she's been home from college. We've got to know what we're talking about on this one."

"I don't think there's any doubt," Slam Duncan interjected quietly, but with a conviction Cramer found compelling. Duncan gestured with his left hand, flashing the Ace bandage that he'd shown up wearing that morning. The computer whiz had mumbled something about a skating accident when Cramer had inquired. Duncan hadn't volunteered more, and Cramer hadn't pursued the matter because his associate was obviously a bit chagrined about the injury. Probably something to do with that attractive young woman Duncan had been squiring around, Cramer thought wryly. The course of young love obviously had a few unexpected and painful turns.

"We've tracked it back now for six months, and cross-referenced it to every operator who's worked here during that time," Duncan was continuing. "It's Ball, all right. Or at least part of the problem is. Here, let me show you."

With a start, Cramer realized he was relieved to let Duncan take the lead in the conference. Cramer was nothing if not perceptive. The esteem in which Ball was held by senior and junior staffers alike had not escaped him, and he had not looked forward to laying out the facts for Posey. But that was part of the job of an auditor, and he had long ago learned to distance himself from it.

No, this was something else. Where his profession was concerned, Cramer let no one in front of him unless the person had earned it. It came as a surprise to discover that the rambunctious, irreverent, outrageous Slam Duncan, over the past two weeks, had somehow sneaked up on the blind side of Cramer's respect. With a smile and a new perspective, he relaxed and for the first time really watched Duncan at work.

"Like I say, we went back six months," Duncan was saying. "We charted the shift of every operator you have in the division. Then we charted the time periods when we know, beyond any doubt, that you had lost computer time. We were able to verify that time had been lost by comparing the logs and repetitive programs that require essentially the same amount of time each time they are run. We found one operator who was on duty on each occasion that you lost computer time. The operator was Don Ball."

"Is there any other explanation?" Posey asked. The resignation in his voice was almost tangible.

"No," Duncan replied. "I wish there was, but there isn't."

"Well, I guess that's that, then. Get it all lined up and we'll have him in after lunch."

"There's one other thing," Duncan said. Cramer sat up expectantly. Duncan had not mentioned to him anything other than the same information he'd given Posey.

"He either doesn't care he's caught, or he wants to be identified. One of these times when there was unauthorized use was just last week, after he was aware we were conducting an audit."

"I'll have him in at 2 o'clock," Posey said. "I'll want both of you here when I confront him."

★   ★   ★

"Yes, sir," Ball said as he strode into Posey's office. "Laurie said you wanted to see me." The words were hardly uttered before the employee caught sight of Cramer and Duncan, seated on the sofa across from Posey's desk. Cramer watched closely. He saw no visible evidence that the presence of the two auditors caused Ball any consternation.

"Sit down, Don," Posey replied. "There's a problem we need to discuss with you. You've met Lenny Cramer and Mr. Duncan, I believe?" Cramer smiled inwardly: It was "Lenny Cramer," but "Mr. Duncan." Looks like the buttoned-down corporation mind-set has taken root with my old friend, he thought. He can't bring himself in a business conference to use a nickname like "Slam" or "Bo".

43

"Yes, I've been talking with both of them for about a week now," Ball responded. "What's the problem?" This time, Cramer noted, there *was* a hint of apprehension in the youngster's voice.

"It seems there has been some unauthorized use of the computer," Posey said sternly. "It has been traced to you, as late as last week. That's pretty serious, Don. It can mean termination. Want to tell me about it?"

Watching Ball's face was like watching a Christmas sparkler fade and die. The brightness ebbed, and nothing but the dry ash of despair remained. The long silence that ensued was broken only by the creak of the sofa as Duncan shifted his weight.

Finally, Ball straightened and said in a a voice low but resolute. "You're right, Mr. Posey. I have been using the system, for about two years now. Not very much, never more than 10 minutes at a time. I'm sorry I did, and it was a stupid thing to do. But I did, and I'll own up to it whether you've got any evidence of it or not."

"How about telling us about it?"

"There's nothing much to tell." Ball was regaining control, and the confidence had returned to his voice.

I like this kid, Cramer thought. It's a shame he had to pull something like this. Let's hope he hasn't been up to some real dirty tricks.

"About two years ago, I purchased some software for a baseball card inventory and value system. That's what I've been doing, updating my baseball card inventory. I only do it on my breaks. That's all."

"That's all! What do you mean, 'That's all?'" Posey said with great agitation. "Don't you know that's a cardinal rule around here! Never bring in any outside programming? My goodness, son, surely you realize what could happen to our system if a virus ever got into it?"

"I know it's against company policy, Mr. Posey." Ball was contrite, but his demeanor was far from hang-dog. He was pleading his case, and doing a pretty good job, Cramer thought. "But I want you to understand. My system at home is secure. Nothing has ever gone into it that didn't come still wrapped in cellophane from the manufacturer. I used brand-new disks to copy the software onto, and that's what I uploaded to our system. I know it doesn't mean anything to you, but I wouldn't even download anything from Coke's computer into mine. Once I worked out the inventory on our system, I went home and duplicated it on mine. I'm sure my system is free of any viruses; I'm not sure about the company's."

"I know you don't have a lot of background in computers. You may not understand that there's almost no way to detect the presence of a virus. Once it gets into a system some way—by being programmed in, or by having it downloaded from somewhere else, you often can't detect it. I know what damage they can do. They can wipe out every bit of programming. They're malevolent, and anybody who'd infect a system with a virus has got to be sick. Anybody who would permit one to get into a system is inexcusably negligent. I know that. I may have been stupid in breaking a company rule, but our system hasn't been compromised because of me. I'll take my licks—I know I've got 'em coming—but you've got greater security problems to worry about."

"What do you mean?" Posey demanded. All three men were immediately alert, intent on what Ball was saying.

"Come on and I'll show you," Ball said, rising.

Just as Ball finished speaking, the phone rang. Posey answered and after a moment said, "Lenny, Slam, how about y'all go check this out. I need to handle this call." Don Ball led Cramer and Duncan to the information systems department.

Walking down the hall Cramer asked, "Aren't you a little old to collect baseball cards?"

Ball's eyes lit up. "Baseball cards are an impressive investment. An academic analysis by a Professor Krause in the late eighties showed that rookie baseball cards were the top investments of the 1980s."

"Baseball cards?" Slam questioned in disbelief.

"Absolutely. A T206 Honus Wagner card from a 1909-11 set, with a crease, sold for $110,000 in 1988. Fewer than 100 of these cards are known to be in existence. The Goudey Gum Company 240-card collection from 1933—including Babe Ruth and Lou Gehrig—sells for about $18,000."

Cramer said, "My mother threw away all of my baseball cards and comic books many years ago."

"That's probably why the old baseball cards are so valuable," Ball replied. "Did you have any DC *Detective Comics*? A complete mint run of *Detective Comics* retails for about $150,000. Over the past five year period the average yearly return has been 36%."

"Holy Bat Caves," Cramer said mockingly. "I used to read Batman and Superman comics. My daughter, however, prefers Wonder Woman."

"Batman, about $47,000 and Superman, say $65,000," Ball stated. "Of course, it's hard to find high-quality investment comics. The acid left in comic book paper during the manufacturing process is the major cause of aging and yellowing."

"Why do you need a computer inventory?" asked Slam.

"So many cards," answered Ball. "A complete *annual* set of every player who goes to spring training camps contains at least 750 cards, costing about $20."

Cramer laughed and said, "Next you'll tell me you sold short Pete Rose cards when they investigated him for gambling."

"Hey, don't laugh. There are even counterfeit Pete Rose cards. You could have sold short Wade Boggs, Steve Garvey—. But let me tell you about the most infamous baseball card ever issued—the 1989 Fleer Bill Pipken card. Number 616."

Ball lowered his voice, "It's the Jesse James of baseball cards. Bill Pipken, a so-so second baseman, posed with an obscenity printed on the knob of his bat. After Fleer wiped the egg off their face, they recalled the pornographic card. It's worse than Claude Raymond posing with his uniform zipper open."

Chapter 7

The several types of statistical sampling plans used by auditors may be generally classified into two categories, attribute sampling plans and variables sampling plans. Attribute sampling is used to obtain a measure of the occurrence rate of a particular characteristic in a population. Variables sampling plans are used to estimate a value range for a characteristic in a population.

— J.W. Cook and G.M. Winkle

The information systems department was a couple of floors below Posey's office. When they arrived, Ball sat down at his computer workstation. The workstation was an IBM microcomputer hardwired to the Coke mainframe. In other words, Ball could run any number of applications at his microcomputer or tie into the mainframe for mainframe applications using his micro as a smart terminal.

Cramer noticed a book, *Standard Catalog of Baseball Cards*, on Ball's desk. He picked up and flipped through a softback book entitled *How to Collect Baseball Cards*, by Krause and Crumbley.

Ball motioned for Cramer and Posey to take a seat. Ball swallowed hard and then said, "Heck, I didn't think updating my inventory occasionally would raise any eyebrows when the higher-ups were using the computer a hundred times more often for their unofficial jobs. Just look at this." At that, Ball's fingers began flying over the keyboard.

After logging in his user-ID, DBALL, and password, FIREBALL, Ball retrieved the mainframe's computer log and displayed it on his microcomputer's monitor screen. The log listed all the jobs run on the Coke mainframe computer for the past 30 days. He pointed to some line items here and there as he scrolled through the log. He said as he pointed, "You can see my inventory activities appear in the log as 'log

47

time,' interruptions between processing of other programs. Of course you already know this. That's how you fingered me, isn't it?"

"Get to your point," Duncan said, getting rather bored looking at the computer log.

"Yes, get to your point," Cramer added, "You said you had something to show us." Cramer removed his phototinted grey glasses in order to see better.

"Well, before I do, I want to know what's in it for me. I don't like squealing on a fellow computer jock, but I just want you to know my game-playing is really insignificant compared to other people's unofficial use of the machine."

"What makes you think you have something we don't already know?" Duncan replied sharply.

"Maybe I don't, but how are you going to know if I don't tell you?" Ball replied cautiously.

"Sure, if you have something really important, we won't make a big deal out of your baseball card inventory. Of course, you'll have to give us a piece of bubblegum. But don't push us, Don. Remember, you're the one in trouble," Cramer said with a frown.

"All right, then, look at this," Ball pointed to the amber screen.

Cramer and Duncan looked. "I don't get it," Duncan said. "That's where somebody ran the online query and search program. What's so unusual or revealing about that?"

"Nothing, if that was the only time," replied Ball. "But look here and here." Ball pointed to a score of similar listings as he continued scrolling down the screen. "The key thing," Ball added as he scrolled and pointed, "is the user ID number. It's not on the registered ID list. It shouldn't work. This person shouldn't be able to do this. He didn't just come up with someone else's valid ID and associated password. He must have gotten in using a trap door. I haven't bothered to see when it started, but he's been doing this for at least the past two years. That's when I first noticed it, anyway. I didn't turn him in because I thought it might be one of my buddies in operations. Later I found out it wasn't."

Duncan interjected, "Well, why didn't you at least bring it up then?"

"Why?" said Ball, "I couldn't see any harm being done. Shoot, it might just be some kid out there hacking. I didn't want anyone to get in trouble over nothing. Besides, when I was in high school I used to hack and tried to break into every computer system I could—just for the fun of it. I never hurt anything. It was just a game with me, as well as some of my friends."

"My point is that this system," continued Ball, "has some real security problems. This illegal entry is just one example of what might be going on all over the system. This log only covers activities in the inventory section of the system, which is where I do most of my programming."

"And your baseball cards inventory," added Duncan in a monotone. His face offered no hint of a smile.

"Right," said Ball with a grimace.

"So what do y'all think?" continued Ball.

"We'll let you know," replied Cramer. "Slam, let's go up to my office and discuss this. Don, we'll get back to you tomorrow." At that, Cramer and Duncan got up and walked out the door, leaving Ball with a solemn look on his face.

"So what do you think?" Cramer asked Duncan as they entered Cramer's temporary workstation at the Coke office.

"Well, the baseball cards inventory is harmless enough, but I can hardly believe Don didn't inform the systems manager of this security problem. I'm going to check into it, but I have a feeling this problem is bigger than just some pimple-faced high school kid hacking. For one thing, a hacker would have been bored to death looking at inventory records long before two years were up."

"I get your point, Slam. What about this 'trap door' thing? As I understand, that's a technique programmers use to get around controls, but exactly how do they do it?"

"It's no big deal, Lenny. When a program is being written or changed, it's possible for a programmer to include some breaks—that is, trap doors—in the program code making it possible to insert additional instructions and to provide intermediate output capability. It's a handy tool for programmers trying to debug a system. Unfortunately, it also makes it possible to insert unauthorized program procedures. These unauthorized procedures facilitate abuse."

Cramer looked puzzled and asked, "Give me an example."

Slam replied, "The best example of a trap door program is what is commonly referred to as a ZAP program. Programmers typically set up a utility ZAP program to modify other programs and data while bypassing controls. Don't get me wrong, a ZAP program can have legitimate uses. Most programmers wouldn't misuse a ZAP program, but the potential is there. The worst part is that the use of a ZAP program leaves few footprints. A 'Trojan Horse' program is another type of trap door. It involves hidden programming code within another program to provide unauthorized entry into a system. Someone appears to have used a 'Trojan Horse' in this case."

"So you think it was a Coke programmer who's been searching the files for who knows what," interrupted Cramer.

"Probably. On the other hand, it could be an outside hacker, although it would take someone knowledgeable about both programming and the Coke computer system to pull it off. Perhaps a former Coke employee," Duncan answered.

"Then it could be an inside job?" asked Cramer.

"Well, yes, but let's not jump to conclusions. I have a few things to check out before I point any fingers. No one is beyond suspicion, even Don Ball. This stunt could be something he's done in addition to his baseball card inventory."

"Wait a doggone minute, Slam. He's the one who told us about this, remember?"

"Hey, it's a possibility. He might figure we can't figure out who the culprit is. Plus, it's a great smokescreen. We're not worried about his extracurricular activities keeping track of baseball cards anymore. Of course, you're right—he's not a likely possibility. My point is—you have to keep your eyes open and not rule anything out. Don't faint, but it could even be your old friend, Posey."

Cramer's mouth dropped open, but before he could speak Duncan slapped him on the back and said, "Just kidding."

"I'm glad. You just don't know what an honorable guy Will Posey really is!" responded Cramer, still taken aback at this lighthearted character assassination of his old friend and current employer.

"No offense, Len, but just remember 'power corrupts and absolute power corrupts absolutely.'"

"I'll buy that as a general rule, but there are individuals in this world who hold honor above petty material gains," said Cramer, feeling a little hostile toward Duncan.

"Whoa, buddy, I can see I've touched a nerve. I guess I'm a little too cynical after my few years as a forensic accountant. I've seen too many upstanding people give in to temptation. It's just something about the computer that tempts some people to assume they can get away with anything. They think just because they do it on the computer, nobody will be able to trace their clandestine activities back to them."

"And often that's a valid assumption because the audit trail gets lost in the computer system." Cramer said, beginning to feel better toward Duncan again.

"Right, old chap. The problem with many computer systems is that the audit trail has not been carefully maintained. Shoot, lots of systems were designed with little or no input from accountants. It's no wonder there's so much computer crime. The average computer crime has been estimated to cost $500,000. Why, the average white-collar crime is only $23,500, and the average armed robbery is even less, only $250. Five hundred grand is a pretty big temptation. What's more amazing is the chance of prosecution is almost nonexistent. Statistics show the bigger the dollar amount of a crime, the smaller its probability of prosecution."

"You must be kidding!"

"I wish I was. It certainly contradicts my idea of justice in America. Hey, we've been jabbering for quite a spell. My dinner alarm clock," said Duncan pointing to his abdomen, "is telling me it's time to go home and chow down."

"You're right. My daughter, Becc, is cooking up something special tonight. You want to join us?"

"Thanks. Amazingly, my busy singles calendar is open, and I'm gonna take you up on that offer."

"Great, you want to ride over with me?"

"Nah, I've my chopper in the parking lot. Can't leave that fine machine unattended after hours. I need to stop at a Starvin' Marvin and get some gas. I'll meet you at your bungalow in an hour—if that's OK?"

"Perfect. See you then," Cramer replied. Duncan stood and walked out of Cramer's office.

As he walked toward his office, Duncan thought that Cramer wasn't such a bad guy for an old professor. Of course, Cramer wasn't really that old; it was just that all professors seemed old. Then he laughed as he thought that was what he was going to be one day—an old professor—if he could ever get his dissertation written. He knew that half the people who start dissertations, never finish them. Well he wasn't going to be in that floundering boat—not after all the hours of coursework he had already invested in his quest for the doctorate degree — the union card to teach at a major university.

★   ★   ★

"Dad, how could you? . . . You didn't bother to call and tell me we were having company for dinner? I've never made lasagna before! What if it's not any good?"

"You're right, Becc, I should have called to ask you if it was OK." Then Cramer sang, "Don't worry, be happy," recalling an old tune that had been playing on the radio lately.

Becc chuckled, "*Please*, Dad, no singing."

"Wait a minute, little girl, you didn't complain when you were a youngster."

"Well, maybe so, but would you put some *real* music on for our dinner guest? You're sure he's not a picky eater?"

Cramer walked from the kitchen and dining area into the living room where his antique armoire stood. He called to Becc, "In the mood for classical?"

"Sure, Dad, anything that goes with lasagna is fine."

The armoire had been converted into an entertainment center. When you opened the doors, a stereo with a CD player and a television were found on shelves inside. Cramer felt this arrangement looked more genteel in his living area. He didn't like having a TV serving as a major focal point in the room. Consequently, a few years ago, he had purchased the armoire at an antique auction and added the shelves later. He was quite pleased with the result. He enjoyed an occasional project which required working with his hands.

Cramer turned on the stereo and selected one of his favorite CDs, one featuring Mozart's five authenticated violin concertos. He then returned to the dining area to help with dinner preparations by setting the table. Becc was still preparing the meal in the adjoining kitchen area. "May I help?" he asked.

"No thanks, *Poppa*, your dinner is almost ready," Becc replied in her Italian accent. "I just hope our guest arrives soon. I'm taking the lasagna out of the oven and it should sit about 15 minutes." Just then the doorbell rang.

Cramer walked over and opened the front door. "Greetings, Sir, please enter my humble abode."

"Why, thank you, my good man. Mmmmm, something smells great. Italian?"

"Indeed, follow me to the dining area and let me introduce you to the chef."

Cramer continued as they entered the dining area, "This is my daughter, Becc, a promising Italian chef."

"Please, Dad, you're embarrassing me. Don't believe my dad until you taste the lasagna. It's my first try."

"Well, as I was saying, this is my daughter, Becc, a worried Italian chef. Becc, this is Slam Duncan, the computer whiz I was telling you about."

"I'm pleased to meet you, Mr. Duncan."

"Slam, please," Duncan interjected. "The pleasure is all mine. And dinner smells great."

"I hope you like lasagna." Becc said.

"I love anything Italian," Duncan responded.

"What would you like to drink, Mr. Duncan, I mean Slam?"

"Water, please."

"Same for me, Becc," added Cramer.

"Let's all go to the table then. We can start on our salad, and I can learn more about the mysterious world of auditing," Becc said with a grin.

As they sat down, Duncan tipped his head to emphasize he was listening. "Mozart, right?"

"Well, now, aren't you the cultured fellow. I knew you were an unusual character. At least a strange combination of computer jock and motorcyclist. I certainly didn't think you had time for the more refined aspects of western civilization." Cramer smiled as he picked up his salad fork.

"Becc, I hope your father has not told you anything about me. I would have thought that he, being an accounting professor, would know we accountants are not the dry little twerps that Hollywood makes us out to be."

Cramer and Becc both laughed. Duncan's almost six and a half foot frame was certainly not little and his personality was far from dry. Becc responded, "All I really know is that you were recommended to Dad and Mr. Posey by an old college buddy named Howie. Dad says you know your stuff, and he's glad you're working with him."

Cramer interrupted with a mouthful of salad, "Now that's all true, except maybe the 'glad' part." Cramer broke into a big grin. He enjoyed kidding around with Duncan. He began to think of himself at Duncan's age, full of vim and vitality, ready to take on the world.

Of course, he was still ready to take on the world; although he had eased off a tad on the vim and vitality stuff. The last few years had been a rough experience, but Duncan was somehow having a rejuvenating effect on him. Funny, how at first, he didn't particularly like Slam's cavalier attitude, not to mention his black motorcycle. Oh, well, sometimes people are not what they first appear to be.

Becc interrupted his "wool gathering." "OK, guys, it's time to dip into the lasagna. Let me serve your portions. The pan is too hot to pass around the table."

"Thanks," said Duncan as he handed Becc his plate. Becc gave Slam a generous slice, and then took her father's plate and did the same. As they took their first bites, she asked, "Well? Well? Don't keep me in suspense!"

"Delicious," responded Duncan while chewing his first bite. "My compliments to the chef."

"Scrumptious, daughter," added Cramer.

"I'm so relieved," said Becc. "You can have all you want. I made a ton."

Later Duncan and Cramer had seconds, and Duncan thirds.

As Mozart's fifth violin concerto entered its finale, Duncan remarked, "Isn't that great. Can you believe he wrote that and his first four violin concertos before he was 20 years old?"

"Yes, he was a genius," stated Becc. "In fact, he wrote all five violin concertos in less than a year.

"Amazing," said Cramer.

"Mozart?" asked Becc.

"No. The way you two have these facts and figures in your heads. All I know is that I like the music."

"Oh, really, Dad. You know all sorts of trivia about Mozart, Beethoven, Bach, and lots of other classical composers."

"Well, I suppose it is true that Schroeder and I consider Ludwig van Beethoven the greatest musician who ever lived. The fact that he was a German composer and possibly a friend of my ancestors has nothing to do with my high regard for his music."

Amused, Duncan asked, "So, you know something about your roots, eh? Well, I'm a wee bit of an highlander myself. No great composers I know of, but there was a great poet from bonny Scotland by the name of Robert Burns."

"Scotland? Well, well, I knew there was something about you I liked," quipped Cramer.

"That's where another branch of our family came from, Slam," joined in Becc. "My great-great-great grandfather came to America in the 1830s. Dad has an old family Bible in which one of our ancestors recorded family events, births and marriages and such."

"Well, that's great," said Slam. "I wish I knew more about my family history; genealogy is fascinating to me. I've heard many stories about my family history, but unfortunately don't have much in writing, like birthdates and marriages. No one seemed to take the time to write down these things in my family. I do know that one ancestor came over in the late 1700s. It seems one of my great-greats supported the attempt of Bonnie Prince Charlie to claim the throne of England. After which things didn't go so well for the Scots, and many left for the Land of Opportunity."

"I know about that from English Literature," added Becc. "He was Prince Charles Edward Stuart. Too bad for him and the Scots, the English brutally beat them at the Battle of Culloden Moor. Mid-1700s, I think?"

"You have English literature in the ninth grade?" asked Duncan.

"Actually it was an advanced literature class back at my junior high in Philadelphia. You learn so much about history from literature, and history is my favorite subject."

"Well, that's only because you haven't had any computer classes yet," Duncan said with a laugh.

"Actually, Slam I've been learning about computers since the sixth grade," responded Becc.

Cramer smiled. "That's right, Slam, old man. The modern generation is learning computers in elementary school. Times, they are a-changing."

"Well, bless my pea-picking soul, I remember reading that kids were using computers in elementary school, but I still find it amazing!"

"Speaking of school, Dad, if you will excuse me, I need to get started on my homework. Can you believe it! School just started and I have a report to write."

"That's fine, dear. I'll get the dishes later."

"I know you will, Dad. Remember our agreement. Just because you brought company home doesn't get you out of it. Good night, Slam. It was nice to meet you. Don't let Dad talk your ears off."

"Nice to meet you, Becc. Dinner was delicious. What's the agreement?"

Cramer joined in, "Whoever cooks doesn't have to clean up. Becc cooked, so I'm the kitchen crew."

Becc interrupted, "Right. I'm glad you liked dinner, Slam. I hope you and Dad have a great audit together at Coke." With that Becc rose from the table and headed to her room.

"You have a great daughter, Len. It must be swell being a father. Although I know it's gotta be hard being a single parent."

"You're right on that one, Slam. I just hope I'm doing an adequate job. There have been some tough times since I lost my wife. Suppose we move into the living room where we can sit back in some easy chairs. Would you like a liquid refreshment? We have coke, lemonade, or milk?"

"Lemonade, please."

As they rose from the table, Cramer said, "Go make yourself comfortable." He pointed toward the living room and then headed toward the refrigerator.

In a minute, Cramer entered the living room holding two tall glasses of ice-clinking lemonade. He said, "it's not a mansion, but it meets our needs."

"It looks a lot better than my bachelor pad. Is that your stereo in the armoire?"

"Yes, you want to take a look?"

"Sure," replied Duncan as he took his lemonade glass. They both walked over to the armoire. The doors were already slightly ajar. Cramer opened them completely.

Cramer began, "I purchased all the stereo components: amp, tape player, turntable, and speakers twenty years ago. Two years ago I acquired the CD player. Would you like to hear something besides Mozart?"

"Do ye have any bag-pipe music for a Scotsman?" Duncan tried his best Scottish accent.

"I should get some," responded Cramer.

"Well, then, just let the violins play," said Duncan.

Cramer motioned to the two easy chairs.

"Ahh, this a comfortable chair," remarked Duncan as he relaxed on the furniture.

"So where are you from besides Scotland, Slam?"

"I grew up in Wayne County, Mississippi. Believe it or not, the Scottish influence was very strong there. The first school in the county was established in 1812 by the Scots. They didn't even speak English. They spoke Gaelic."

"I know a little about Gaelic. Eighteen letters in the alphabet, compared to English's twenty-six."

"That's right. One old Scotsman, Sir George MacKenzie, said, "our pronunciation is like ourselves, fiery, abrupt, sprightly, and bold."

Cramer added, "The Scots were a tough, thrifty, hard-working people. They made good pioneers. They were fiercely independent, possessed a strong love of family and country, and had stern moral values."

"Hmmm, haven't changed much have they, Lenny?"

"No, I guess not. There's a movement in Scotland even now to separate from Great Britain. Apparently many of them feel they didn't get their fair share of the North Sea oil revenues."

"Are you serious? Could they really separate from Great Britain? The South tried to separate from the U.S. in the American Civil War. The results weren't too good."

Cramer answered, "It's a different situation in Britain. Scotland and England were separate countries for most of their history. They fought many a bloody battle with each other before joining together as the United Kingdom of Great Britain. The British flag, the Union Jack, is a combination of the old Scottish and English flags."

Cramer continued, "One issue of British pound notes features a picture of Robert the Bruce, the Scottish king who thoroughly whipped the English at the Battle of Bannockburn in the 1300s. I saw the battlefield during some free time while attending a conference at the University of Stirling. It seems that the English executed one of Scotland's major heroes, William Wallace. As a result, the Scots were pretty fired up by the time the English army made it to Bannockburn."

"I bet," laughed Duncan. "Of course the original Scots had already made a mark on history as fierce warriors."

"You mean the Picts," interjected Cramer. "The Romans may have conquered Europe, but the Roman emperor, Hadrian, had to build a wall to protect Roman Britain from the northern tribes."

"Besides being tough soldiers, the Scots are renowned as engineers," added Duncan.

"Precisely why the starship Enterprise's chief engineer was Montgomery Scot," said Cramer recalling his favorite TV reruns.

"So you're a Trekkie?" asked Duncan.

"I like science fiction and roller coasters," replied Cramer.

"Strange combination. Not too many years ago, computers were science fiction," said Duncan. "The first computers were used in business in the late 1950s."

"The first generation," added Cramer. "In class, my students have to identify the characteristics of first, second, and third generation computers."

"Let me try, Lenny. Vacuum tubes, transistors, and integrated circuitry or chip technology. And some say the fourth generation is marked by large scale integration."

"Forgive me, Slam. You're the computer expert. Why am I telling you about computers? You get an A-plus on your quiz. How would you like to make a guest lecture to my classes sometime this semester?"

"That could be fun. Let's plan on it."

"Good. We'll arrange a time later. Students really appreciate speakers who can share some real-world experiences."

"Well, Lenny, your consulting work should keep you loaded with 'war stories' to share in class."

"That's true. I feel it is unfortunate that most new professors don't have time for consulting or practicing part-time. Too much research pressure. Publish or perish, that's the name of the game today. Like most things in life, there needs to be a balance. Emphasis on research should be balanced by an equal emphasis on teaching."

"I believe that. Remember, I'm in a doctoral program. It's incredible how much I had to read. There's so much in the accounting literature now, so much theoretical stuff with little practical application that I can see."

"Let's face it, Slam, only professors and professors-to-be read much of the academic research. Of course, some of it makes a useful contribution. A doctoral program is somewhat like fraternity initiation, except mental hazing seems to be permitted."

"I would laugh, but I think you're right, Len. I will be glad to get the dissertation behind me. Some people told me I shouldn't be taking time out to do anything else, like this consulting job. But, hey, I gotta eat."

"I'm glad you did, Slam. I really need your help on this Coke job. What do you think we should tell Don Ball tomorrow? Whatever we decide, I'll discuss with Will."

"Personally, I don't have a problem with his baseball card program. He seemed to be doing his job. Instead of a coffee break, he simply took a baseball card break. On the other hand, he should not have loaded the program into the Coke system. That should be a strict no-no. He could have kept the program on a disk and used it on his microcomputer. The worst thing he did in my judgment is not informing his superior about the apparent break-in by the person with the unlisted ID. For now, why don't you just tell Ball that he's officially reprimanded and not to use the computer for unofficial business any more?"

"Sounds reasonable. I'll discuss it with Will in the morning. It appears Coke needs more specific written policies on controls and security. As far I can tell, Ball didn't break any written rules."

"Good documentation of controls is essential to an efficient accounting information system," added Slam. "The programs, control procedures, run manuals, and the like need to be well documented and kept up-to-date."

"What do you think about this apparent hacker? Did he get in through a trap door? And if so, is he a Coke employee or an outsider?"

"Lenny, I have a suspicion, and once I check it out, I'll get back to you. There are a number of people who could do it, but why is still the big question. If the hacker limited himself to Ball's department, all he's looking at are inventory records."

"Could he have sent himself some supplies and then resold them?" asked Cramer.

"I don't think so. Coke has a good separation of duties between record keeping and physical custody of assets. Shipping would have to approve that type of transaction, and the hacker wouldn't have the necessary authorization to get that approval. So, I don't think that would work."

Duncan continued, "Uh, oh," as he noticed the clock on the wall. "I'm afraid I've taken advantage of your hospitality. It's time for me to be moseying on home. I have had a great time. Nothing like a home-cooked meal, a much-needed break from bacheloring."

"Well, now, don't rush off, Slam. I've thoroughly enjoyed our conversation."

Duncan eased himself up from his chair after setting his empty glass on a side table. "No, I've gotta go get my beauty sleep. Thanks a heap for everything. I'll holler at you first thing in the morning."

Cramer rose and followed Duncan to the door. "I'm really glad I met her. Be sure to tell her again how much I enjoyed the lasagna."

"I'm glad you came over and Becc really enjoyed meeting you, too."

"Good night," Duncan said as he opened the door.

"Good night, easy-rider," quipped Cramer as he watched Duncan walk toward the motorcycle parked in his driveway. "An interesting character, that Slam," thought Cramer as he closed the door. "This audit might be more fun than I first thought." Cramer picked up the two empty lemonade glasses and headed into the dining room. After clearing the table, he started for Becc's room to tell her good night, but the phone rang before he left the kitchen.

"Hello," he answered, wondering who would call this late.

"What? How? I can hardly believe it, Will. Yes, I'll come by tomorrow." Cramer hung up the phone and thought his little operational audit was becoming rather complicated. The Coke computer system had come down with a pesky virus. "Tomorrow is going to be a tough day," he thought. He went by Becc's room. She was doing her home-work with stereo headphones on. He told her good night. Later, in his room, he took a long time falling asleep. He kept thinking that he was overlooking something.

Chapter 8

Many executives seem to be infatuated with the limitless information potential of computers—sometimes at the real expense of the human thinking that ought to be at the base of any analysis. When playing the enticing "what if" games that computers make available, beware contracting "spreadsheetitis." And remember, machines cannot think (not yet)—they can only rearrange what was furnished them previously.

— Philip Kropatkin

Cramer was always amazed by the impeccable neatness of Posey's office. The desk was always organized. Only a few papers lay on the desktop; apparently they related to the crisis at hand. Next to the main desk was a smaller desk. On it was a Bentley Model T microcomputer, a color monitor, and an Epson printer. Cramer noticed the computer was not running. He recalled that Posey once said, "If there's another way to do it, why use a computer?"

Cramer then noticed the photograph on Posey's desk. It was a family picture of Will, his wife, and two daughters. Momentarily, Cramer's heart ached for his wife. He supposed that he would never really get over missing her. Amazing, how fast the memories returned.

"Will, you look like death warmed over. Didn't you sleep well?" Lenny Cramer asked.

"Ha. Sleep? I wish. Computer people from the main office had me up here most of the night. We've been trying to get the system back up. As I told you last night, everything went down. Looks like we may have lost some files."

"Let's start at the beginning, Will. What happened to the computer system? What caused it to go down?"

"It was a virus. The night operator indicated that there was a problem about six yesterday evening. By 7:30, things were getting out of control, so he called the systems manager at home. She came up here soon afterwards. She then called in the analysts from our main office about 10 o'clock. I called you soon after that. The virus caused my subsystem"—Posey waved his right arm—"that is, overseas development, to crash first. Next, the inventory data base went down. A couple of other systems were slightly affected before we got things under control."

Lenny knew firsthand what a virus could do. Virus programs instruct the host computer to summon stored files. When it does so, the virus program copies itself onto the files. Consequently, the computer's memory degenerates into a big mess. Hackers sometimes create viruses to show off their skills.

"How did it get in?" asked Cramer.

"Apparently, someone uploaded it from outside using a modem. You ought to go talk to the systems manager for the details."

Just then Posey's phone rang. He answered, "Send him in." In a moment Duncan opened the door.

Before Cramer or Posey could speak, Duncan spoke in a rough imitation of John Wayne. "Well, pilgrims, we'd best circle the wagons. We're under attack."

Posey tried to smile and said, "I'd laugh if I could."

"Slam, I'm afraid our employer hasn't had enough rest. I guess you've gotten the scoop."

"Just that a nasty bug seems to have infected our modern technology. Lucky for Coke they already have on hand two of the world's leading computer consultants."

"Where . . . ." began Cramer before realizing Duncan was referring to the two of them. "Well, I wish I had so much self-confidence, Slam. This audit is turning into a little bigger problem than I've had to deal with before."

Cramer continued as he looked at Slam, "We need to go talk to the systems manager and find out exactly what happened." Cramer turned back to Posey and said, "Last night Slam and I discussed our smaller problem of Don Ball. He seems like a pretty decent fellow. We recommend you send him a reprimand letter with a warning not to update his baseball cards inventory or other games on company time. Additionally, you should send a memo to all appropriate personnel not to run unauthorized programs on Coke computers."

"Fine, I will. In the meantime, you computer whizzes can go give my computer a shot of something and get my system back up. More importantly, you can help me revise it so something like this doesn't happen again."

Cramer and Duncan both left Posey's office. They arranged an appointment with the systems manager later that morning. After the meeting with the systems manager, Cramer and Duncan went to Cramer's work area in the Coke building to discuss the meeting.

"So what do you think, Lenny? Does the systems manager really have everything under control?"

"He seems competent enough to me. I do appreciate his attitude toward hackers who load viruses into computer systems."

"Lock them up and throw away the key!" Duncan laughed. "You remember the big virus incident in November 1988?"

"Oh, sure, the Cornell graduate student who managed to shut down 6,000 computers around the country. The computers were connected through ARPAnet and other E-mail networks in the Internet loop. Some of the nation's top science and research centers were affected. That incident surely made a lot of people start thinking about computer security."

Cramer continued, "The worst part is that the guy became a hero to several thousand computer jocks. You know the type I mean. The ones who see security measures as challenges to break. A lot of press coverage focused on admiration of the guy's handiwork, but not his ethics. Some people tried to downplay the seriousness of what he did by explaining that his program was not a virus that destroys data, but a worm that simply uses up storage space. Whatever you want to call it, the bug stopped computer operations at centers all around the country. The creator of a virus can't be sure that it won't get out of control and destroy important data somewhere in a computer network."

"I couldn't agree more." Duncan broke into the lecture. "Whether it's a virus program or a worm program, it's a major headache for system users. Admittedly though, a virus that destroys irreplaceable data is much worse than a worm that simply brings the system to a halt."

Cramer nodded. "Looks like the Coke system was affected by a virus. But at least there was a backup for most of the data files that were destroyed."

"This type of incident is alarming to the external auditors. No doubt they'll be concerned about the system's internal controls when they discover that this occurred."

"Good point, Slam. I'm lecturing on the auditor's responsibility for internal control tomorrow in my auditing class. Which reminds me, when are you going to speak? How about next week?"

"Fine. If it's OK with you, I'll discuss the problem of hackers getting into computer systems? That particular issue has been on my mind lately, if ya know whudda mean, Vern?" asked Duncan, trying to imitate comedian, Jim Varney and inject a little humor.

Cramer grinned. "Perfect. That will fit in nicely with the chapter on EDP auditing which the students are assigned to read in the textbook."

Cramer glanced at the CompuAdd personal computer on his desk and said, "Let's see if we can link to the mainframe system. The systems manager said it would be up and running by now."

Cramer loaded his terminal emulation software into his microcomputer. The screen then displayed the same log on message that a "dumb" terminal would display. Cramer's microcomputer was effectively a "smart" terminal. In other words, it could send and receive information like a dumb terminal connected to the mainframe, but it also could do some processing. The processing ability is what made it a smart terminal. One particularly useful feature of using a microcomputer as a smart terminal was the ability to upload and download files between the mainframe and the micro.

"What the ...!" Cramer gasped after he typed in his user ID, LCRAMER, and then his password, SCOTLAND. User IDs were assigned by the Coke Systems Department, but users selected their own passwords. The screen displayed the following message:

LENNY CRAMER, QUIT THE AUDIT OR
YOUR NEXT LECTURE WILL BE YOUR LAST!!

Duncan's brow knotted as his eyes focused on Cramer's monitor screen. "Someone's gotta lot of nerve," Duncan flatly stated. "Either someone has a warped sense of humor, or this audit is becoming rather serious. Looks like we've scared someone."

"Apparently so," said Cramer in a slightly shaky voice. His throat was dry and his pulse was racing. He wanted to appear more at ease than he felt. "I don't like being threatened," he said with bravado.

Cramer continued speaking. "Professors don't usually have to deal with this sort of problem. I think I'll review all the workpapers, and see if I've overlooked something. I'm sure as heck not going to resign from the audit. What really puzzles me is what have we done to upset someone so much? We haven't found anything really bad. I guess we must be close to something, though."

"That's a good idea, Len. Take a second look at everything we've done so far. Do you think we should inform the local authorities about this threat?"

"No, I don't want to do that. I'd have to withdraw from the engagement then. Remember, I'm just starting up in Atlanta. I need the money. Coke wouldn't want the publicity. Let's just keep this message between the two of us. At least for now. Agreed?"

"Gosh, old buddy, are you sure? This threat seems to have me more worried than you."

Cramer was feeling more comfortable again. His pulse had slowed back to normal. "I'm sure, Slam. I doubt whoever made this anonymous threat has any intention to carry it out. Most people who threaten are just bluffing. So, do you agree to keep it confidential?"

"You're the boss. I need the money, too. I just hope we're doing the right thing."

With that Duncan walked to the door. Cramer followed him.

"I'll see you tomorrow, Slam."

"OK. I'm going to do some more examination of the password security system. I think I'm close to figuring out who's been doing the unauthorized searches in the inventory system. After your threat, I'm more anxious than ever to know. It could be related."

"We'll see," said Cramer. At that Cramer returned to his desk. As he did so, Duncan watched with concern. He wondered if silence was the right thing? Should the cops be called? Well, he had given his word. He wouldn't tell anyone without informing Lenny first. He stopped fretting and walked away from Cramer's office. He headed toward his work center. When he arrived, he turned on his microcomputer and logged on the mainframe.

"Well, well," he said to himself. "I'm glad I wasn't left out." The screen bore the message:

BEAUREGARD DUNCAN,
QUIT THE AUDIT WHILE YOU CAN
OR YOUR NEXT COMPUTER LOG ON
WILL BE YOUR LAST!!

A grim expression came over his face. "This is getting a little too personal. I won't put up with harassment," he thought angrily. He settled back in his chair and noticed his clenched fists. He laughed slowly.

Those fighting instincts were still there. No matter how civilized a person was, just underneath the surface was the deadliest animal on planet Earth. The human brain had made man the dominant species, and Duncan knew he would have to use his if he was to find the person behind this threat. As adrenalin pumped through his biosystem, he actually felt invigorated by this personal challenge from some anonymous person.

As with Cramer's message, Duncan knew there was no way to trace it. Both messages were too personal to be random messages. The culprit knew that Cramer was a professor, and that Duncan was something of a computer jock. Since he couldn't get any fingerprints from the message, he cleared the screen and went to work. Hours passed.

*　　*　　*

After the anonymous warning to quit the audit, Cramer worked the rest of the day trying to deduce who sent it. He thought much about the matter as he drove slowly up Martin Luther King's Freeway in the Atlanta rush hour traffic. Based on the workpaper review, no one seemed to be seriously threatened by his audit. Maybe that was the answer. It wasn't in the workpapers. As Slam had indicated, perhaps it was tied to the unauthorized searches in the inventory system by the presumed hacker. The hacker was also suspected of the virus incident.

Cramer continued thinking of the day's events. After the initial shock, the threat really didn't worry Cramer all that much. He had seen too much of life to be bothered greatly. He had faced other difficult circumstances, particularly the loss of his wife. He recalled his wild experience in Burma last year, and a Bible verse came into his mind. "Those who hope in the Lord will renew their strength. They will soar on wings like eagles; they will run and not grow weary, they will walk and not be faint."

He mused how life could bring a person some difficult circumstances, and he was thankful that his God was bigger than any problem he would face. That thought was particularly reassuring to a single parent.

He pulled into the driveway, turned off the ignition, and walked to the door. As he unlocked and opened the door, he didn't hear Becc. "Becc," he called. No answer. "Lord, protect us," he thought as he walked faster than usual to her bedroom. He looked in the doorway.

She looked up, stereo headphones on her head. "Hi, Dad," she said cheerily. "How was your day?" she asked, removing the headphones.

"Fine," he answered, breathing more easily. "Let's go get burgers for dinner. OK?"

"I would rather have chicken. Are you feeling well?"

"Yes, the traffic was rougher than usual." He lied. "I'm going to change, then we'll go get burgers *and* chicken." He turned away from her doorway and walked to his room. He thought, "I'll be glad when this audit is over!"

★   ★   ★

"Margaret Barbera was very good with numbers. She could take a balance sheet, a set of account books, invoices, bills, and more, juggle and manipulate the figures and, presto, thousands became millions, losses became profits, profits became losses, sales soared or fell, whatever her employer desired, and it would take an expert auditor knowing precisely where to look and what to look for to figure out what she'd done, and even then, it still might slip by." Professor Cramer was in front of his auditing class quoting a passage from *The CBS Murders*, by Richard Hammer.

He liked to start off each of his auditing classes with something provocative from real life. The twenty-six older students, mostly women, were sitting in small, time-worn chairs in a room with pale-white paint peeling from the walls.

Cramer continued the passage. "There is an underground of people like Margaret Barbera, eagerly sought after by businessmen in trouble, especially in volatile and unstable industries, such as garments and jewelry. Ask the right questions of the right people, and pretty soon a Margaret Barbera, or somebody very much like her, will come knocking at the door."

As he tossed the softback book back into his briefcase, he glanced out of the window. He saw street people strolling by outside. The auditing class had started at 5:30 in the general classroom building on the Georgia State University campus. He thought, "The word campus may not be the best description of Georgia State. Combat zone, maybe." Being on the quarter system, this auditing class met twice a week, two hours and fifteen minutes per class. Cramer was a subway stop professor, a part-time professor.

As he walked over to place his first overhead slide onto the projector, he saw that it was bolted to the table. He chuckled softly. The glass top was dusty, so he leaned over and blew the dust from the antique projector.

"Wisdom is knowing what to do; virtue is doing it," Cramer said. "Just saying you believe something isn't enough. You have to take action to prove those beliefs are valid. You've all heard the expression that talk is cheap. Anyone can learn how to talk the talk, but it takes dedication to walk the walk. Today we're going to discuss a crucial element of the auditing profession, of any profession, and that crucial element is ethics."

Cramer continued. "Individual responsibility is the critical issue in establishing a code of conduct. A code of professional conduct is formulated to provide a minimum level of conduct for the well-being of a profession. The American Institute of CPAs' Code of Professional Conduct describes the responsibility of the CPA to colleagues, clients, and the general public."

A student raised his hand, and Cramer responded. "Yes, you have a question, Ralph?"

"Not a question, exactly, Dr. Cramer. But it seems to me that it's a waste of time talking about ethics. Everyone knows you can't teach ethics and morality. Everyone's already made up their minds about those things before they get to college."

"Perhaps," said Cramer. "Supposedly college students still have an open mind. But whether your personal code of ethics parallels the Institute's is irrelevant. Either you follow the profession's code, or you get expelled from the AICPA."

Cramer added, "In fact, one reason we have a professional code of conduct is to provide some uniformity in the way different CPAs respond to similar situations. There are four distinct parts of the AICPA's Code: Principles of Professional Conduct, Rules of Conduct, Interpretations of Rules of Conduct, and Ethics Rulings."

Cramer placed an overhead transparency on the projector. The transparency listed the six principles of professional conduct:

1. *Responsibilities*. In carrying out their responsibilities as professionals, members should exercise sensitive professional and moral judgments in all their activities.

2. *The Public Interest*. Members should accept the obligation to act in a way that will serve the public interest, honor the public trust, and demonstrate commitment to professionalism.

3. *Integrity.* To maintain and broaden public confidence, members should perform all professional responsibilities with the highest sense of integrity.

4. *Objectivity and Independence.* A member should maintain objectivity and be free of conflicts of interest in discharging professional responsibilities. A member in public practice should be independent in fact and appearance when providing auditing and other attestation services.

5. *Due Care.* A member should observe the profession's technical and ethical standards, strive continually to improve competence and the quality of services, and discharge professional responsibility to the best of the member's ability.

6. *Scope and Nature of Services.* A member in public practice should observe the Principles of the Code of Professional Conduct in determining the scope and nature of services to be provided.

Cramer pointed to the screen and continued his discourse. "These principles should be the basis of everything a CPA does. These basic principles were carefully evaluated by the Institute when the other three parts of the Code were established. Also, when a CPA encounters a situation in which there is no specific Rule of Conduct, Interpretation, or Ethics Ruling, then the CPA must be guided by these principles."

"The Rules of Conduct provide the minimum levels of acceptable conduct. They are enforced by the Ethics Division of the AICPA. The Interpretations and Ethics Rulings provide more detailed guidance."

Another student raised a hand. "Yes," Cramer responded.

"I understand these are guidelines, but what actually happens to a CPA who breaks a rule?" An older student asked.

"It depends on the specifics of each individual case," Cramer replied. He then pulled out an old issue of *The CPA Letter* which contained the Semiannual Report of Joint Ethics Enforcement Program Activity. As he glanced at the dog-eared document, he said, "For example, in the last six months of 1987, the Ethics Committee disposed of 239 case investigations. Of those 239, 143 resulted in no violation findings, 31 in minor violation letters, and 26 in administrative reprimands. The remaining 29 investigations were either being prepared for or were submitted to the Trial Board."

The student interrupted. "What did the Trial Board do?"

Cramer frowned at the interruption. He was a stickler for students raising their hands. He continued with a frown at the student. "Well, during that same six-month period, the Trial Board expelled seven and suspended two members under automatic provision of bylaws. For example, being sentenced to a year or more in jail results in automatic expulsion. At Trial Board hearings, two members were suspended and required to take some CPE—uh, continuing professional education. Three members were admonished and required to take some CPE."

Cramer placed another overhead on the projector. "These are the Rules of Conduct." The screen showed Rules 101 to 505.

INDEPENDENCE, INTEGRITY, AND OBJECTIVITY
101 Independence
102 Integrity and Objectivity

COMPETENCE AND TECHNICAL STANDARDS
201 General Standards
202 Compliance with Standards
203 Accounting Principles

RESPONSIBILITY TO CLIENTS
301 Confidential Client Information
302 Contingent Fees

OTHER RESPONSIBILITIES AND PRACTICES
501 Acts Discreditable
502 Advertising and Other Forms of Solicitation
503 Commissions
504 Form of Practice and Name

After Cramer placed the overhead transparency on the projector, a student raised her hand. "Yes, Beth," he acknowledged along with a nod of his head.

"What happened to the 400's?" she asked.

"Good question. The 400 series related to encroaching on the practice of colleagues. Those rules were determined to be in restraint of trade and have been suspended at this time."

"An area closely related to ethics is what should the auditors do if they become aware of an illegal act committed by the client firm's personnel. Guidance for the auditor's action is found in SAS No. 54, *Illegal Acts by Clients*, and SAS No. 53, *The Auditor's Responsibility to Detect and Report Errors or Irregularities*. Is the auditor expected to find illegal acts?"

When no one raised his hand, Cramer called on the first student who made eye contact. "Joyce?"

"Well, Dr. Cramer, I'm not sure, but it seems to me that they would only be expected to find the illegal act if it had a material effect on the financial statements."

"Excellent, Joyce. You are absolutely correct. Consider this scenario. You're auditing a computer manufacturer, and you're sampling the sales invoices and discover sales of microcomputers with the latest technology to Vladimir Rocket company in Tripoli, Libya. Is there a problem?"

Joyce raised her hand.

"Yes, Joyce," Cramer responded.

"I don't know this for sure, but I suspect we're not supposed to conduct business with countries like Libya. You know—terrorist city." The other students laughed.

"Good point. The CPA should make inquiries of the client's management concerning compliance with laws and regulations and preventive measures used by the client to prevent illegal acts. In addition to inquiries, there are other audit procedures that may detect illegal acts. For example, an illegal act may be discovered during compliance tests used to assess control risk, related tests of transactions and balances, and inquiries of the client's legal counsel. The illegal act may be the selling of technology to banned countries or as mundane as fraud by one of the client's personnel. Back to the question, what should you do as the auditor?"

"Call the cops," someone yelled. The class roared with laughter.

Cramer smiled. "Not exactly." Cramer read from the textbook, *Auditing Concepts, Standards, and Procedures* by Hubbard, Johnson, O'Callaghan, and Pushkin. "I'm reading from our textbook, Chapter 17. When the auditor's examination provides evidence that illegal acts may have occurred, the auditor should: (1) consider the implications of the act and its effect on the statements, (2) consult with the client's legal counsel, (3) report the incident to a sufficiently high level of management and the client's audit committee, and (4) consider performing additional auditing procedures, if practical or possible."

"A disclaimer of opinion is generally issued by the auditor if the CPA is unable to obtain sufficient competent evidence regarding a possible illegal act. However, if the auditor concludes that an illegal act has occurred that is material and believes disclosure should be made in the statements, a qualified or adverse opinion should be expressed if disclosure is not made. A qualified opinion or disclaimer should be expressed if the auditor is unable to reasonably estimate the effect the illegal act has on the statements."

"Even if an illegal act is not considered material by the CPA, the auditor should request that management take appropriate remedial action. If management refuses to do so, the auditor should consider withdrawing from the present engagement and possibly severing any future relationship with the client. It is the duty of management, not the auditor, to notify outside parties of illegal acts committed by the client. End of quote."

Cramer discussed a few more cases before dismissing class. After class Cramer thought about his upcoming trip to Washington. He had been requested to appear at a Congressional hearing concerning the integrity of the accounting profession. Cramer sincerely hoped the profession would indeed abide by a high code of ethics. Failure to do so would surely cause the end of the profession's self-regulation. "The last thing this country needs," Cramer said to himself, "is another government agency, especially one to regulate the accounting profession."

Cramer left the classroom building. He felt a grumpy mood coming over him as he walked to his car. "I'm going to cheer myself up before I get home and see Becc," he thought as he got in his car to drive home.

When he arrived home, he found Becc watching a Star Trek episode on TV. "Which do you like the best, the old shows or the new ones?" he asked as he walked into the living room. Cramer always enjoyed discussing the merits of the various characters among the two closely related TV series. He was inwardly pleased that Becc had become a major fan of the crews of both captains, Kirk and Picard.

"Gee, Dad, that's hard to determine. Last time we talked about this I picked the new series, but lately I've been watching your videotapes of the old ones. I really like that eposide called 'City on the Edge of Forever.'"

"Oh, yeah, that's my favorite episode! McCoy goes through a time portal called the 'Guardian of Forever' and accidentally changes history. Kirk and Spock go after him. They wind up on Earth during the 1930's. Kirk falls in love with a character played by Jane Seymour."

"That's it. Do you remember that hysterical scene where Kirk explains to the police officer how Spock's ears became pointed?"

Cramer and Becc both grinned.

Becc's grin faded abruptly. She said, "There were a lot of humorous moments in that episode, but the ending was so sad! Why, I almost cried."

"The ending was very solemn, but all Trekkies know that it's James T. Kirk's love for his ship, the Enterprise, that keeps him going during moments of despair."

Father and daughter talked for another half hour about Star Trek before calling it a night. Cramer wasn't looking forward to the next day. Tomorrow morning, he was scheduled to appear in court as an accounting expert witness. He felt restless, but strangely fell asleep almost the instant his head hit the pillow.

Chapter 9

Taking a job with a nationally recognized public accounting firm has provided many fast trackers with a solid career foundation. It offers the experience needed to sit for the CPA exam and provides an overview and technical expertise not always available at a smaller practice.

— Arielle Emmett

Cramer woke early. He was anxious about his court battle, which was scheduled first thing this morning. Even though he had served as an expert witness on other occasions, there were always some butterflies before appearing in court. "Last minute jitters," he thought. "Some people claim a little nervousness helps you do a better job."

Cramer had a light breakfast with Becc. She said goodbye and left for school, leaving Cramer alone to ponder his court case. He decided to take a cab. He thought, "I could drive, but why fight the traffic if the attorneys who hired me will reimburse me anyway? I'm sure they'd want me to have a clear head, not one that's been muddled by Atlanta traffic. I can look over my notes on the ride downtown, too." The attorney's client was a CPA firm which was being sued by a group of disgruntled ex-stockholders. They were ex-stockholders because their former investment had gone belly-up. They contended that the CPA firm had failed to perform the audit properly. Cramer called a local cab company, and in a few minutes he was riding into downtown.

"Everyone wants to sue the CPA firm," thought Cramer as he rode along unconcerned with the traffic problems confronting the cabbie.

Cramer began to ponder the litigation problem of American society. "The lawsuit problem had gotten worse in recent years. The underlying context of a lawsuit against accountants is almost always a client firm's financial disaster. An external user of the audited financial statements—a creditor or investor— has lost money. The only suffering on the part of the accountant is possibly an unpaid bill. Thus, they are the only ones who have not financially suffered from the disaster. They are also still solvent, and are often perceived as having 'deep pockets.' As a result, they are obvious lawsuit targets, because if one does win a judgment against the accountants, the judgment is collectible. Civil damage suits against professionals were rare until the mid 1960s. At that time an outbreak of civil malpractice suits were aimed first at physicians, then at accountants and lawyers."

Cramer slowly shook his head as he continued pondering the problem. "Much of the legal liability crisis is due to a tort system which may be out of control. Innocent victims of negligence should, of course, be fairly compensated for economic damages, but society cannot afford the costs of protecting everyone from his own folly."

He remembered a case in which a youth was paralyzed when he fell through a roof while burglarizing a school. The award he received was largely due to school officials having several prior warnings of the roof's dangerous condition. This particular incident seemed to indicate a need to return common sense to the law. "Should someone willfully doing wrong, in this case burglarizing, be given an award?" Cramer asked himself.

Cramer was so lost in thought that the cab ride seemed to take no time. After paying the cabbie, he walked quickly up the courthouse steps. Following a brief greeting from the attorney outside the courtroom, he was soon on the witness stand.

"Professor Cramer, for the court's record, please state your full name and current address."

"Paul Leonard Cramer, the third, 1601 Elizabeth Avenue, Atlanta, Georgia."

"Dr. Cramer, we wish to thank you for testifying today as an expert witness about certain accounting matters. First, I have several questions for you concerning your background. Where did you obtain your Ph.D. degree?"

"University of Illinois."

"Where did you receive your MBA degree?"

"Harvard University."

"Where did you receive your bachelor's degree?"

"University of Massachusetts at Amherst."

"Are you listed in Who's Who in America?"

"Yes."

"What years were you president of the American Accounting Association?"

"That was 1994-95."

Lenny had rehearsed most of these questions and answers before. Lenny liked the grueling task of preparing beforehand and participating in a courtroom battle over accounting principles. There was the challenge to react and respond to the many trick questions asked by the opposing attorney. Probably the stress was not worth the daily fees he received, but he loved it. He sometimes imagined the opposing attorney to be an aggressive college wrestler anxious to pin him to the rubber mat. Not one of those actors-wrestlers you see on television late at night on professional wrestling. Lenny always pinned his vicious opponent in his daydreams.

"Professor Cramer, have you written any accounting books?"

"I have written four accounting books. One principles of accounting textbook, a forensic accounting book, an auditing handbook, plus an accounting casebook for MBA students."

"Would you please explain what is meant by forensic accounting?"

"Briefly, forensic accounting is a science that deals with the relation and application of accounting facts to business and social problems." Lenny smiled and turned toward the jury. "As I tell my students, a forensic accountant is like the Columbo or Quincy characters of yesteryear, except he uses accounting records and facts to uncover fraud, missing assets, insider tradings, and other white-collar crimes." Lenny turned back to the pinstriped lawyer.

"Dr. Cramer, where are you currently employed?"

"I am the Glenn Fess Professor of Auditing, Georgia State University."

"Is it an honor to hold a professorship?"

"Yes, there are few professorships in accounting." Lenny thought, "Yes, no money, just a title. The real money is in a 'chair' designation." Lenny was still searching for a chair designation at an agreeable university.

"Professor Cramer, are you a Certified Public Accountant?"

"Yes, in Pennsylvania, since 1970," Lenny responded.

"Are you a member of the American Institute of CPAs?"

"Yes, since 1970."

"Do you serve on the Board of Directors of any major corporations?"

"Yes, I serve on the Board of Directors of three of the top Fortune one hundred companies and for three smaller companies."

"Dr. Cramer, are you an outside consultant?"

"Yes, I have my own forensic accounting firm here in Atlanta."

76

"Please estimate how many professional articles you have written."

"About 75." Lenny shifted in the wooden chair.

"Uh." The attorney shuffled several pages and then continued, "have you ever appeared as an expert witness in the courtroom?"

"Yes. I have been an expert witness for accounting matters on about twelve different occasions—three oil companies, two banks, one insurance company, a manufacturing company, an accounting firm, the Internal Revenue Service, the SEC, and two divorce cases."

"What is the SEC?"

"Sorry. The SEC refers to the Securities and Exchange Commission. The SEC was created by the Securities Exchange Act of 1934. It has the legal authority to prescribe accounting methods for firms whose shares of stock and bonds are sold to the investing public on the stock exchanges. The law requires that such companies make reports to the SEC, giving detailed information about their operations. The SEC regulates the amount and type of information to be included in annual and quarterly reports and the methods to be used to develop the information. For the most part, the SEC has followed the standards established by the FASB concerning the methods used to develop the required information."

"What is the FASB?" the young-looking lawyer asked.

"FASB stands for the Financial Accounting Standards Board that began to issue standards in 1973. The SEC has charged this seven-member independent nongovernmental body with the responsibility of developing and issuing standards of financial accounting affecting the private sector of the United States. Committee members include public and nonpublic accountants as well as non-accountants. In short, the FASB is our current source of Generally Accepted Accounting Principles for which accountants use the acronym GAAP."

The well-dressed attorney turned to the judge and said, "Your honor, we present to this court Dr. Cramer, as an expert witness in the area of forensic accounting and auditing."

The robed judge turned to the opposing attorney and said, "Mr. Groomer, do you have any objections to this request?"

The opposing attorney stood up and spoke loudly, "No, your honor."

"So moved. You may proceed, counselor."

Lenny answered a number of technical questions that he had previously rehearsed. Then the opposing attorney began his questioning. His questions focused on audit samplings for tests of transactions. The class-action negligence battle was brought by shareholders of QQQQ, Inc., an electronics-store chain, against their accounting firm, Peat, Andersen & Whinney. The chain's former management was accused of creating "phantom" inventory and profits.

"Now, Dr. Cramer, would you tell the court how an auditor statistically determines if the accounting records of a firm like QQQQ, Inc., are correct?"

Cramer continued. "Compliance tests are used to verify that a particular control procedure is working properly. For example, many business firms have procedures to ensure that they don't pay twice for the same order of goods from a vendor. Generally, this procedure would involve accumulating documents like the purchase requisition, purchase order, receiving report, and the bill or invoice from the vendor. After comparing the data on all these documents to verify agreement, then a payment voucher would be prepared. All these documents would be forwarded to the firm's treasurer for check preparation. When the check is prepared, all these documents would be stamped 'paid.'"

Cramer paused to take a sip of water from the glass he had poured earlier. "The procedure I just described would ensure that if a firm received two bills for the same order, that the firm would not pay both times. The process also ensures that only goods actually ordered and received are paid for. The process of accumulating the documents into a voucher package and stamping them 'paid' when the check is written is a control procedure which an auditor may choose to test."

The attorney looked puzzled. "Are you saying, Professor Cramer, that the auditor may not test this procedure?"

Cramer was not surprised by this question. He thought to himself, "The general public knows so little about the true purpose of an audit. Perhaps worse than the public's mere ignorance was the public's misperception of what an audit is supposed to do. That misperception was usually referred to as the 'expectations gap.'"

"Professor Cramer, please answer the question." The attorney broke Cramer's train of thought.

"No, the auditor does not have to test any particular internal control procedure, only those upon which the auditor chooses to rely. Depending on the firm's unique situation, the auditor may rely upon many or no controls. After the auditor reviews the internal control system, a requirement of any audit, then the auditor selects those controls upon which he or she plans to rely. These controls will then be tested to see if they are functioning properly. The extent to which the auditor can rely upon these controls will determine the extent of the auditor's substantive tests."

"Professor Cramer, could you explain substantive tests?"

"Substantive tests are also referred to as tests of detail. Their purpose is to detect material misstatements in the client firm's financial statements. The auditor must design substantive tests to determine if recorded book values are reasonably stated or if they are materially misstated. For example, a substantive test may estimate the dollar error in an account balance or class of related transactions, such as the dollar error in the accounts receivable balance or in the recorded total for sales. They also may be used to estimate an unknown account balance."

Lenny paused for a moment to get his breath and then continued. "The quantity and quality of substantive tests are related to the field work standards. The *first* standard of field work mandates that substantive tests be adequately planned and properly supervised. The *second* standard requires that the nature, extent, and timing of substantive testing be based on the assessed level of control risk. The *third* standard requires that substantive tests contribute to the necessary sufficient competent evidence upon which to base an opinion regarding the financial statements under investigation."

"Now the risk that the auditor will reach the wrong conclusion is comprised of three separate risks: environmental risk, control risk, and detection risk. Perhaps I can discuss these risks later." Lenny looked directly at the attorney.

"As I was saying, however, before performing *substantive* tests, the auditor reviews the internal control structure, selects controls on which he or she plans to rely, and then tests those controls. The tests of controls are called compliance tests because these tests determine if the client firm's personnel are following, that is, complying with, the firm's stated control procedures."

"Before we go any further, I would like to review the basic steps in the audit process. May I?"

The attorney frowned, but said, "Go ahead."

"First, the auditor plans the audit. This step includes gathering information about the client's firm and industry conditions. Second, the auditor studies, tests, and evaluates the client firm's control structure. Third, the auditor performs and evaluates substantive tests. The second and third steps are the evidence-gathering steps of the audit. Audit working papers are used to document the auditor's techniques. Based upon this evidence, the auditor completes the fourth and final essential step, issuing the audit report."

"The auditor's standard report is comprised of three paragraphs. I have made several copies for your perusal." Lenny reached down and opened his briefcase. He removed several pages. On each was a copy of the auditor's standard report as shown below.

Board of Directors and Shareholders
XYZ Corporation

Independent Auditor's Report

We have audited the accompanying balance sheets of XYZ Corporation as of December 31, 1990 and 1989, and the related statements of income, retained earnings, and cash flows for the years then ended. These financial statements are the responsibility of the company's management. Our responsibility is to express an opinion on these financial statements based on our audits.

We conducted our audits in accordance with generally accepted auditing standards. Those standards require that we plan and perform the audit to obtain reasonable assurance about whether the financial statements are free of material misstatement. An audit includes examining, on a test basis, evidence supporting the amounts and disclosures in the financial statements. An audit also includes assessing the accounting principles used and significant estimates made by management, as well as evaluating the overall financial statement presentation. We believe that our audits provide a reasonable basis for our opinion.

In our opinion, the financial statements referred to above present fairly, in all material respects, the financial position of XYZ Corporation at December 31, 1990 and 1989, and the results of its operations and its cash flows for the years then ended in conformity with generally accepted accounting principles.

Smith and Jones
Certified Public Accountants

Cramer continued. "This standard report includes what is referred to as an 'unqualified opinion,' which basically means that the financial statements are fairly presented. This standard report would be issued at the conclusion of any financial statement audit, unless there was a situation requiring a modification."

"Such as?" the attorney interrupted.

"There are basically two situations requiring an opinion other than an unqualified opinion. One, if there is a limitation on the scope of the auditor's work. Two, if the financial statements are not prepared in accordance with GAAP applied on a consistent basis."

"Speak in laymen's terms please," the attorney said in a huff.

"Excuse me. GAAP is generally accepted accounting principles. GAAP is referred to in the auditor's report."

"Please explain this scope limitation."

"As shown in the report, the auditor states that the audit was made in accordance with GAAS, that is, generally accepted auditing standards. In situations where the auditor does not follow generally accepted auditing standards or is unable to perform auditing procedures which he or she considers necessary, the standard report must be modified to reflect this limitation in the scope of the auditor's work. The auditor can issue either a disclaimer or a qualified opinion. If the auditor disclaims an opinion because of a scope limitation, the audit report will contain only three paragraphs. The first paragraph would state that the auditor was engaged to audit the financial statements, which are the responsibility of management. The second paragraph would discuss the nature of the scope limitation. The third paragraph would disclaim an opinion. If the auditor disclaims an opinion, the auditor does not discuss what an audit is since this explanation may overshadow the disclaimer."

"The nature and potential effect of the scope limitation determine whether the auditor should issue a disclaimer or a qualified opinion. For an example of a disclaimer opinion due to a scope limitation assume that the client did not take a physical inventory of merchandise at year-end for 19x2 and 19x1 and that no evidence is available to support the cost of property and equipment acquired prior to December 31, 19x1. Based on this information, the auditor's disclaimer of opinion might read as follows:"

Independent Auditor's Report

We were engaged to audit the accompanying balance sheets of X Company as of December 31, 19x2 and 19x1, and the related statements of income, retained earnings, and cash flows for the years then ended. These financial statements are the responsibility of the company's management.

(Second paragraph of standard report should be omitted)

The company did not make a count of its physical inventory in 19x2 and 19x1, stated in the accompanying financial statements at $_____ as of December 31, 19x2, and at $_____ as of December 31, 19x1. Further, evidence supporting the cost of property and equipment acquired prior to December 31, 19x1, is no longer available. The company's records do not permit the application of other auditing procedures to inventories or property and equipment.

Since the company did not take physical inventories and we were not able to apply other auditing procedures to satisfy ourselves as to inventory quantities and the cost of property and equipment, the scope of our work was not sufficient to enable us to express, and we do not express, an opinion on the financial statements.

"If the auditor's scope is limited and the auditor decides not to disclaim an opinion, the auditor should issue a report which is qualified because of a scope limitation. The third paragraph of the auditor's report would express an opinion that the financial statements are fairly presented in accordance with GAAP, except for any adjustments which may have been required had the auditor been able to complete the audit without any scope limitations."

Cramer paused to take two sips of water from his glass. "Departures from GAAP can result in a qualified or an adverse opinion. Would you like further explanation?"

The attorney stared at Cramer for a couple of moments. "Not at this time. Let's go back to the issue of compliance tests and substantive tests. In particular, I would like for you to explain the statistical approaches that auditors use."

"Sure. Let's go back to my previous example of stamping the documents in the voucher package 'paid' when the check is prepared to pay the vendor's invoice. This procedure ensures that the firm only pays once for each vendor's invoice, and then only for goods which were actually ordered and received. The documents in the voucher package confirm goods were ordered, with the purchaser order, and confirm goods were received, with the receiving report. The person making out the payment voucher would examine these documents to be sure that they agreed with one another."

"If this procedure was not followed, the accuracy of the financial statements could be impaired. For example, the cost of goods sold amount on the income statement is often calculated by adding net purchases to beginning inventory and subtracting ending inventory. The amount of purchases is based on the payments to vendors for goods ordered. If those payments, that is, the checks, are not properly prepared, then cost of goods sold could be overstated or understated. Most likely overstated, since the vendors would probably complain if they did not receive payment for the goods shipped, but may not complain if they received over-payment."

Cramer paused and looked around the room. He possessed a professor's habit of periodically making eye contact with his audience. He noticed that the judge seemed to be half-asleep. He sighed and started to continue his lecture. Before he could begin, the attorney interrupted.

"Excuse me, Dr. Cramer. Your Honor, I would like to request a short recess."

The judge seemed to perk up a little bit. "A good suggestion. The court will recess for 15 minutes." He slammed the gavel. Everyone filed out of the courtroom. Most headed for bathrooms or concessions. Cramer followed a small group to the public phones.

After waiting several minutes for a phone to become available, he got one and dialed Slam's number at the Coke building. Cramer could not have imagined what was happening at the other end of the phone line.

"What am I doing?" Slam thought. He was leaning very far out the window of his office when the ringing phone startled him. "Man, oh, man, I must be working too hard," he thought as he walked to his desk and picked up the phone.

"Slam, what took you so long?" came the voice over the phone even before Slam could say hello.

"Lenny, it's weird. I was daydreaming and looking out my window."

"Right, Slam. So you were daydreaming while I'm downtown busting my buns in a witness box at the courthouse. All the while, I'm counting on my colleague, Slam Duncan—computer whiz—to make some serious headway on our operational audit. I called to check in, and he tells me he's having a weird daydream!" Lenny's voice rose a few decibels as he finished his rebuff to Slam.

"No, no, you got this all wrong, Len. I think I'm seriously freaking out," Slam pleaded, although he was a little offended at Lenny's lack of compassion. Slam continued. "Your phone call must have brought me back to reality. I was leaning out the window but I can't remember how I got there. In fact I can't remember what I was thinking. No, wait a minute. I remember...I was flying. I thought I was a bird!"

"Weird, very weird, partner. You're sure you're really on the level?" Lenny became concerned. He felt bad about his initial gruffness. "But," he thought, "who wouldn't be a little grumpy after sitting around a courthouse all morning?"

Lenny continued. "Look, Slam, go over to your computer. Check out the program you're running. I think someone may be sending you subliminal suggestions."

"Now who's weird? Are you serious?"

"Yeah. I'm really serious. I've done some reading on the subject. A subliminal suggestion is a message flashed on a screen too fast for conscious reading. The television industry outlawed subliminal suggestions years ago. You may recall a Columbo episode some years ago dealing with subliminal suggestion. Also one of the new Mission Impossible episodes dealt with the subject."

"Just go check out your computer. I gotta go. They're calling everyone back into the courtroom."

Lenny hung up the phone and joined the crowd milling around outside the courtroom door. He had an uneasy feeling about Slam.

Just as everyone found their seats, the bailiff had everyone stand for the judge to enter the room. Lenny mentally prepared himself for the attorney's questioning.

"Professor Cramer, could you continue with your explanation of how auditors test control procedures. You were discussing the process of stamping the voucher package as 'paid.'"

"To test the control that the voucher package is stamped 'paid' before a check is issued, the auditor could retrieve each check and associated voucher package. If the stamp was missing, then the auditor would know the control procedure failed, that is, the client personnel did not follow the firm's stated procedures."

"Due to the large number of transactions, the auditor would be unable to examine every transaction in the population of all purchase transactions. The cost of examining every transaction would be too great for the firm to pay. Thus, to test the control, the auditor would select a sample of purchase transactions. The auditor would then retrieve copies of the associated voucher packages to determine if the documents were stamped."

"This type of sampling is known as attribute sampling. In this case, the attribute being tested is the stamp on the voucher package documents. The auditor can use either *statistical* sampling or *judgmental* sampling. If statistical sampling is used, the auditor can mathematically determine the sample size by using either a formula, a graph, or a table, and randomly select the sample items. The auditor next investigates each sample item and prepares a working paper showing the results of the investigation. The auditor can then make a statistical conclusion about the effectiveness of a control procedure. Mathematical methods are used to determine sample size and to objectively justify its adequacy. This means that the sample findings are free of unintended bias and defensible. The statistical approach provides a basis for expanding subsequent audit procedures if the results of a statistical test indicate that such expansion is necessary in the circumstances. Statistical sampling allows the quantification and control of sampling risks.

The attorney frowned. "What do you mean by sampling risks?"

"Whether you use statistical or judgmental, that is, nonstatistical sampling, there are two types of sampling risk associated with attribute sampling. They are: one, the risk of underreliance and two, the risk of overreliance. Underreliance risk is associated with the risk that sample results will indicate control ineffectiveness when in fact the true rate of breakdown is acceptable for the auditor's assessment of control risk. Auditors refer to the risk of underreliance as alpha risk. Auditors say that a Type I error results when a sample evaluation indicates that an effective control is ineffective."

"The risk of overreliance is defined as the beta risk and a Type II error occurs when the sample evaluation indicates that an ineffective control is effective. The auditor does not know when a Type II error occurs because the auditor has erroneously concluded that a control is functioning properly. The opposite is true for a Type I error, that is the auditor does not know when a Type I error occurs because the auditor has incorrectly concluded that a control is not working properly."

"In addition to sampling risks, there are nonsampling risks. These risks can be controlled by auditor competence, proper planning and supervision, and the CPA's adherence to appropriate quality control standards. The greater the degree of auditor competency, proper planning and supervision, and adherence to high quality control standards, the less the nonsampling risk."

"Guidelines for sampling are provided in SAS 39, uh, Statement on Auditing Standards Number 39, Audit Sampling. SAS 39 was issued by the AICPA, uh, American Institute of CPAs in 1982."

"Allow me to go over a brief example of a compliance test using attribute sampling. Let's continue with our earlier example. Assume there are 5,000 purchase transactions each year, and the auditor wishes to determine that there is a stamped voucher package associated with each check disbursed. The auditor wishes to select a sample from the population of 5,000 transactions. Assume that the auditor wishes to be 95 percent sure of the result, that is, there is a one in twenty chance that the sample will misrepresent the population."

"In addition to the reliability level, in this case 95 percent, the auditor must also specify the tolerable rate of occurrence, TRO. In other words, the auditor must use professional judgment and determine how many deviations or lapses from the control procedure could occur without materially affecting the financial statements. Let us assume the auditor sets the TRO at 10 percent."

"Last, the auditor must estimate the expected rate of occurrence, ERO. That is, what error rate does the auditor expect to find. Typically, the ERO is based on prior experience, such as from previous audits. For this example, the auditor sets ERO at five percent."

"Tables exist to aid the auditor in determining sample size for attributes. Table 1 is an example." Cramer stopped to hand out two pages from his briefcase. One was marked Table 1 and the other, Table 2. Cramer resumed his discourse. "Table 1 shows sample sizes for various tolerable rates of occurrence and various expected percentage rates of occurrence when the reliability is 95 percent. By examining this table, the auditor will determine that the sample size should be 120."

"Assume the auditor randomly samples 120 payroll calculations and finds errors in six calculations—a 5 percent sample occurrence rate. Once the auditor has found the rate of occurrence in the sample, other tables are consulted to determine the achieved upper precision limit given the specified reliability. Specifically, Table 2 can be used to evaluate the findings."

"In this example, the sample size is 120, so find 120 in left-most column of Table 2; the number of occurrences is 6; find 6 in the same row that has sample size of 120. Thus, the upper precision is 10 percent

Table 1
Determination of Sample Size
When Reliability = 95 Percent

Expected percent rate of occurrence	Tolerable rate of occurrence										
	1	2	3	4	5	6	7	8	9	10	12
0.50	*	320	160	120	100	80	70	60	60	50	40
1.0		600	260	160	100	80	70	60	60	50	40
2.0			900	300	200	140	90	80	70	50	40
3.0				*	400	200	160	100	90	80	60
5.0					*	500	240	160	120	80
7.0							*	600	300	140
10.0											800
15.0											
20.0											

* = MORE THAN 1,000.

Note: This table is exact for sampling with replacement and is a conservative approximation for sampling without replacement. It is designed for large populations where sample size is less than 10 percent of the population.

Source: Adapted from Ernst & Ernst Professional Development Series, Audit Sampling Reference Manual, 1974, p. 16.

found at the top of the column containing occurrence rate of 6. Thus, the auditor can be 95 percent assured that the population error rate will not exceed 10 percent. This is same as the 10 percent originally deemed to be tolerable."

"The other type of audit tests, substantive tests, are associated with variables sampling. Auditors use attribute sampling for compliance testing of control procedures. Variables sampling is used for substantive testing to estimate the dollar reasonableness of a financial statement account balance or the amount of material misstatement if the account is not reasonably stated. Auditors may use several types of variables sampling plans in conducting an audit. No one type of sampling plan is appropriate in all circumstances."

"SAS No. 39, Audit Sampling, and SAS No. 47, *Audit Risk and Materiality in Conducting an Audit*, discuss the risks associated with

Table 2
Evaluation of Sample Results Where
Reliability is Present at 95 Percent

NUMBER OF OBSERVED OCCURRENCES (DEVIATIONS)

UPPER PRECISION LIMIT: PERCENT RATE OF OCCURRENCE

Sample Size	1	2	3	4	5	6	7	8	9	10	12
30										0	
60				0			1				2
100			0		1		2	3	4		6
120			0	1		2	3	4	5	6	8
200		0	1	3	4	6	7	9	11	12	16
300	0	1	3	6	8	11	13	16	18	21	26
500	1	4	8	12	16	21	25	29	34	38	47

Note: This table is exact for sampling with replacement and is a conservative approximation for sampling without replacement. It is designed for large populations where sample size is less than 10 percent of the population.

Source: Ernst & Ernst Professional Development Series, Audit Sampling Reference Manual, 1974, p. 21.

substantive testing. According to SAS No. 47 the audit risk that is related to an individual account or class or transactions on the financial statements is the product of the following risks: (1) that environmental factors, before evaluating the functioning of internal control, will lead to material error—'inherent risk,' (2) that the system of internal control will not prevent material error or detect it on a timely basis—'control risk,' and (3) that the auditor's procedures will fail to identify a material error not identified by the internal control system-'detection risk.'"

Cramer paused to clear his throat. "If you will bear with me, I have two more handouts for you. These will show how the auditor selects a variables sample to estimate the difference between a firm's recorded book value for an asset, such as inventory, and its true value." Cramer reached in his briefcase and handed out pages containing the following information.

The auditor has been assigned a variables sampling job to determine the reasonableness of the client's inventory balance. The auditor has previously observed the year-end count and was satisfied as to the count and the summarization of the count on the inventory summary sheets. The auditor prepares an audit program in which he randomly selects a sample of inventory items listed on the inventory summary sheets and traces those items to appropriate vendor invoices, comparing the unit prices on the inventory summary sheets with the unit prices on the vendor invoices.

The auditor, in the audit program, specified the risk levels for incorrect rejection and incorrect acceptance at 20 and 20 percent, respectively, and indicated that the tolerable amount of error in the account should be 5 percent of the inventory account balance. Based on the prior year's working paper, a $10 standard deviation of differences was to be used in calculating the sample size.

The auditor will use the sample to estimate the difference between the client's recorded values and the audited values. This difference will then be used to estimate the true value of the population, in this case, that's inventory. The formula for calculating the sample size for the difference estimator is as follows:

$$n = [s(Z_{alpha} + Z_{beta})/(Min/N)]^2$$

where:

n = sample size

s = estimated sample standard deviation

Z_{alpha} = factor from the normal table for a two-sided alpha risk (risk of incorrect rejection)

Z_{beta} = factor from the normal table for a one-sided beta risk (risk of incorrect acceptance)

Min = minimum amount considered material

N = population size

After everyone received the pages, Cramer continued his lecture. "The first item needed is the standard deviation, in this case, $10. Next, we need the Z-values for alpha and beta risk. Alpha risk is a two-sided test; thus, when we look up the Z-value in the table of Z-values associated with the area under the normal curve. To do this, we would take half the alpha risk, in this case, half of .20 or .10, and subtract that from half the area under the curve or .50. The result is .40. We would then look up the Z-value associated with .40; the answer is 1.28."

The attorney looked puzzled. "Professor, I studied statistics many years ago. What is a Z-value?"

"The Z-value is the number of standard deviation units associated with a given area under the normal curve from the mean value. For example, plus or minus three standard deviations from the population mean of a normal distribution includes 99.9 percent of the population values, plus or minus two standard deviations includes 95.4 percent, and plus or minus one standard deviation includes 68.3 percent."

The attorney looked slightly less puzzled and nodded his head. "Please continue."

"The Z-value for the beta risk is a one-sided test; thus, you subtract the whole beta risk amount, 20 percent, from .50. The result is .30. Consequently the Z-value for the beta risk is 0.84. Depending on the level of alpha and beta risk the auditor wishes to use, these Z-values will vary."

Cramer paused. He noticed the people in the room had disinterested looks on their faces, but he continued with his lecture anyway. "The next item in the formula is the minimum amount the auditor considers material. Let us assume the inventory is listed at $100,000; thus, five percent is $5,000. Also, let us assume the population size is 2,000 items. By inserting these amounts in the sample size formula, the sample size is determined to be 72 items. The auditor would then select the 72 items from among the population of 2,000 items to estimate the difference between the true value and the client firm's recorded value."

Cramer stopped. He thought, "These people have no idea what I'm talking about. Oh well, I have to try."

The attorney asked, "Could you continue this example all the way to the auditor's conclusion?"

"Certainly. Assume the auditor takes a sample of 72 items and compares his audited value to the client's recorded book value for each item. The auditor determines that the book value of all 72 items is $720 more than the total audited value. Thus, the estimated population difference is calculated by multiplying the average difference of $10 by all 2,000 items in the population. The auditor's point estimate value for the population would be the book value of $100,000 plus the difference of minus $20,000. In this case the auditor's point estimate value is $80,000. However, to quantify the probability of this being the true value of the inventory, the auditor must establish a precision interval around this point estimate."

"To calculate the precision interval, we must know the standard deviation of the sample. Assume this standard deviation is determined to be $9. This amount is used to calculate the standard error. You divide the standard deviation by the square root of the sample size, in this case, the square root of 72. The standard error is, therefore, $1.06. The formula for the precision interval is N times the Z-value for alpha risk times the standard error. In this case, the precision interval is 2,000 times 1.28 times $1.06, which equals $2,715. Thus, the auditor concludes with 80 percent confidence that the true inventory value is $80,000 plus or minus $2,715.

Since the client's recorded book value of $100,000 is not within the decision interval, $82,715 to $77,285; the auditor must statistically conclude with 80 percent reliability that the inventory account is not reasonably stated."

"Thank you for that lecture on statistics, Professor Cramer. I feel confident that all of us have benefited." The attorney smirked. He then turned to face the judge. "Your honor, could we please have a short recess at this time?"

The judge frowned and looked at his watch. "The court will recess for an hour for lunch." The judge's gavel slammed and the judge abruptly left the courtroom. He appeared to have heard enough about audit sampling.

Cramer beat the crowd from the courtroom and was the first to reach the public telephones. He quickly dialed Slam's number. After one ring, Slam picked up the phone.

"Yes." Slam's voice came over the phone line. Cramer breathed a sigh of relief.

"That you, Len?"

"You got him. So you didn't fly out the window. Was the computer involved in your odd behavior?"

"You were right, Sherlock. I used a memory-resident program, that's a program that runs concurrently with another program. I used the memory-resident program to slow down processing of the program I was running before my daydream. That's when I saw it. Parts of the subliminal message would appear on the screen for a split second. When the program ran at normal speed I couldn't see it. But when I slowed down the processing speed, there it was."

"Was what? What was the message?"

"You can fly. Soar like an eagle."

"And you believed that!" Lenny laughed now that he was no longer worried.

"The amazing part is how the bum managed to get this message to appear mixed in with the program I was running. This message would appear only a word or two at a time along with pictures."

"Pictures?"

"Yeah. Pictures of birds in flight. I guess I thought I was ready to join them. You know, Lenny, this is one unusual audit. I'm not sure you're paying me enough. By the way, the same subliminal message was on your computer."

Lenny chuckled. "We'll talk about your pay later. Besides, maybe we'll write a good novel when we catch the bad guy. I have to get back to the trial." He paused. "Slam, I'm glad you're all right. See you later."

"Okay."

They hung up the phones simultaneously.

Lenny didn't feel much like eating, but needed to kill some time before returning to the courtroom. He walked outside the building and found a little bookstore. He browsed there for a while. Afterwards he bought a sandwich at a delicatessen. As he ate, he wondered who had sent the subliminal messages to Slam.

Following his light lunch, he returned to the courthouse. Shortly, everyone involved had resumed their former positions in the courtroom.

The attorney whispered to the assisting attorney on his left and then turned back to Cramer. "Professor Cramer, help me out with a calculation. Assume the client firm has inventory stated at $4,039,000. The auditor wishes to estimate the inventory value based on the following sample data. One, the sample size is 100; two, the standard deviation of the sample is $200; three, the mean of the sample is $4,000; and four, there are 1,000 items in the population. Shouldn't the auditor reject the recorded book value if it's not between $4,000,000 plus or minus $25,600?"

Cramer pulled out a pen, a piece of paper, and his calculator. He typed in the formula: 1,000 times 1.28 times $200 divided by the square root of 100. The result was $25,600. He said, "Yes, the precision interval is plus or minus $25,600."

The attorney smiled; so did the assistant attorney. Cramer was puzzled by their expressions of apparent satisfaction.

"So, Professor, the auditors are wrong if they accept a recorded book value of $4,039,000?" The attorney's face had a look of pleasant anticipation, but it was quickly replaced with a frown when Cramer answered.

"No, no. I see what you're driving at. But the auditor may not have made a mistake accepting a value of $4,039,000. He may have used a different confidence level than 80 percent, such as 90 or 95 percent. The Z-value, also called reliability coefficient, is 1.28 for 80 percent confidence, 1.65 for 90 percent, and 1.96 for 95 percent. If you use the 95 percent confidence level, then the auditor would derive a wider precision interval. Let's see ... It would be 1,000 times 1.96 times $200 divided by the square root of 100."

Cramer keyed the amounts into his calculator. "The answer is $39,200. Thus, $4,039,000 would be between auditor's upper precision limit of $4,039,200 and lower precision limit of $3,960,800."

The attorney shook his head. "This is really confusing me. How could an auditor reach different conclusions using the same data?"

"Let me explain. By widening the decision interval from plus or minus $25,600 to plus or minus $39,200, the auditor increases the confidence level from 80 to 95 percent. The real question the auditor must ask is whether plus or minus $39,200 is sufficiently accurate. But being 80 percent confident that the true value is between $4,000,000 plus or minus $25,600 is equivalent to being 95 percent sure that the true value is between $4,000,000 plus or minus $39,200."

A light seemed to go on inside the attorney's head. He looked disappointed. "Okay, I see your point. The auditor could accept the $4,039,000 value depending on how precise he needed to be."

"Yes."

"Well, how does the auditor determine the level of precision required?"

"In auditing we use a term called materiality. Materiality relates to the maximum amount a financial statement item could be misstated without affecting a financial statement user's decision process. Precision in statistical sampling corresponds to materiality. For example, consider a scenario in which an investor is considering purchasing stock in a firm with the inventory amount we just discussed, that is, $4,000,000. The question that the auditor must ask is what is the minimum amount of change that would affect the investor's decision. Would a change of $25,000 affect the investor's decision? $30,000? $40,000? $400,000? The answer is the level of materiality."

"If the level of materiality is determined to be $40,000, then the auditor must conduct the audit to ensure at least that degree of accuracy."

"Professor Cramer, how does the auditor determine this level of materiality? It seems very important as it corresponds to precision in statistical sampling?"

"A very good question and there is no easy answer. The CPA must exercise professional judgment in determining the level of materiality. Depending on each client's unique situation, the level of materiality may be different among audits by the same CPA firm."

"How does the auditor gain this professional judgment? By passing the CPA exam?"

"Not exactly. Passing the CPA exam is the first step. However, to become a licensed CPA, one must also attain a certain level of experience. One or more years of work under the supervision of a CPA are required. The experience requirement varies from state to state.

"How can you be sure that a CPA firm is exercising good professional judgment in statistical sampling, and in conducting the audit, in general?"

Cramer shrugged off a feeling of defensiveness. He knew it was the attorney's job to question the work of CPAs who conducted the audit. If they were found negligent in conducting the audit, then the attorney and his clients—the ex-stockholders—would win the lawsuit. Cramer could be objective in his responses to the attorney's questions since he truly did not know whether or not the CPAs had been negligent. However, he assumed innocence till proven guilty.

"In 1988, the AICPA established a quality review program for all members in public practice. Prior to 1988, many CPA firms were already participating in a quality review program. CPA firms that are members of the AICPA's Private Practices Section or the SEC Practices Section are required to have a quality control manual and undergo peer review. This program was started in 1977; prior to that time, CPA firms could participate in a voluntary quality review program."

"Who performs this peer review."

"The quality review programs are conducted by firms of comparable size and practice. The Quality Control Standards Committee of the AICPA has identified nine elements of quality control in *Statement on Quality Control Standards No. 1*. These elements pertain to independence, assigning personnel to engagements, supervision, professional development, and acceptance and continuance of clients. If you like, I can look up the other elements."

"No thanks, professor. You've made your point."

A few more minor questions followed before Lenny's testimony was complete. From his previous experience as an expert witness, he had learned to restate the interrogator's question to suit his own purpose. He was pleased that things went so smoothly.

Following some small talk with some acquaintances, Cramer hailed a cab to go to his office at Georgia State. On the way he read an article on expert systems for auditors in *Financial and Accounting Systems*. Expert systems were just one of the latest computer tools available to assist auditors. He was planning a class lecture on the topic. He recalled expert systems were the subject of Slam's dissertation. After his recent experience, however, Slam might wish to consider the topic of subliminal persuasion.

CHAPTER 10

Traditionally, the time of criminal acts is measured in minutes, hours, days, weeks, months, and years. Today some crimes are being perpetrated in less than 0.003 of a second (3 milliseconds). Thus, automated crime must be considered in terms of a new time scale because of the speed of the execution of instructions in computers.
— W. Thomas Porter and William E. Perry

Slam was in a terrible emotional state. He knew what the problem was. He had moved into the realm of love with Laura.

Yes, the state beyond liking. Sure he had liked several other women. But not love. Not that totally vulnerable world of love. Slam spoke out loud. "I'm not a teenager. Why can't I handle this? Because love is a dangerous emotional feeling. Dangerous?" He was now actually hearing the words in the songs on the radio. That was a new experience for Slam. When he heard certain songs, he would think of Laura and get goosebumps. He thought that goosebumps at his age were ridiculous.

If he were driving down Martin Luther King Freeway and heard certain songs, his chest would swell up. He would begin waving his hand and arm in rhythm with the music. Yes, dangerous if someone thought he was motioning to them.

Slam was awaking earlier in the morning. He would wake up in the middle of the night. He needed less sleep. Was this a common reaction to love?

Besides, what was love? Slam began typing a letter to Laura on his word processor.

"I am entering the world of love. It is a totally new experience for me. I have no ground rules. I do not know how to behave." He stopped for a moment.

"Please be understanding," he continued typing. "I may do something stupid or silly in my efforts to impress you. Please forgive me if I do."

Slam stopped typing and read what he had written. He punched the delete button. The screen went blank.

Why was it that women could write love letters, but most men could not? Why were men afraid to put their emotions on a blank piece of paper? Afraid of blackmail? Unmanly? Too frightening? Too exposed?

Slam had tried before to express his emotions to Laura. He had cut out some pictures and cartoons from the newspaper.

He had folded several pieces of white paper and made a booklet. On the front he wrote "Top Secret." Inside he drew a funny face with the statement "Slam likes Laura."

How juvenile it was. One cut-out of Ben Franklin said "Laura is beautiful." And she was.

With another clipping of two shoes, Slam wrote "I would walk 100 miles for Laura." He made little trails of red dots around the shoes. One of the trails of dots ended with the statement "I got lost here."

*   *   *

Cramer had precious little break time between the Coke audit and his auditing class at Georgia State, not to mention his serving as an expert witness. When he did have a spare minute he tried to catch up on the local news by reading the paper. The feature story in the *Atlanta Constitution* was a perennial one—abortion. Atlanta had received quite a bit of notoriety on the issue. In earlier incidents, the Atlanta cops had apparently been a bit brutal hauling away the "Operation Rescue" pro-life protesters. Very unfavorable news photos of the Atlanta police force in action had appeared in news reports all over the country. There was even a case where a Catholic priest who had been arrested at the protest, was later thrown in solitary confinement for the "crime" of offering Mass while in an Atlanta prison. News accounts were comparing the Operation Rescue actions to the Civil Rights protests of the 1960s.

Thinking about the peaceful protesters brought back memories of Cramer's early days. His old friend, Will Posey, had been involved in the Civil Rights movement. Many years had elapsed since those care-free college days. It was interesting how Will had brought them back together by hiring him to do the operational audit for Coke. He had first met Will at a conference for collegiate accounting societies at the University of Illinois. By chance, he and Cramer were involved together in several workshops and immediately became friends. Lenny was an undergraduate accounting major at the University of Massachusetts in Amherst at the time. Will was attending Grambling State University, a predominantly black school in Grambling, Louisiana. Both Lenny and Will were highly enthusiastic about the field of accounting. Both had grand dreams about the future of the profession and the impact they personally would make. Later, they both were accepted to the M.B.A. program at Harvard. There they became truly close friends while learning to properly pronounce "hah-vuhd" and having numerous Boston adventures together.

Cramer went on to pursue a doctorate at the University of Illinois. After earning his Harvard M.B.A., Will accepted a job with the Internal Revenue Service. Later he switched to his present job with Coke. They stayed in touch through the years, mostly through Christmas cards. Will had helped tremendously with Cramer's move to Atlanta. The more he thought about the old times, the more he wanted to have a non-business related meeting with Will. He rose from the dining table where he was reading the paper and found his address book. He looked up Will's home phone number and called. An answering machine received his call.

After the typical "beep," he began his message. "Will, old buddy. It's Lenny. Guess what? I have to quit the audit! Just kidding. Let's get together for lunch as soon as possible. We have a lot of catching up to do." He hated talking on those machines. He left his work and home phone numbers and hung up. He then realized that he was late in leaving for his class.

★　　★　　★

Lenny Cramer hurried into the old, white block general classroom building. He was already late, so he did not have time to go to his office. Instead he headed toward the waiting auditing students. He wanted to talk about the seven types of audit evidence today.

They were physical examination, confirmation, documentation, observation, inquiries from clients, mechanical accuracy, and analytical tests. As Cramer walked into his classroom he noticed that the overhead projector was already on, and he chuckled when he saw a fallen down stick figure on the screen. It was labeled Lenny Cramer. Scrawled across the top of the screen was:

AUDITORS NEVER DIE.
THEY JUST LOSE THEIR BALANCE!

Cramer then noticed a group of students at the front of the classroom. As he walked toward the front he asked loudly, "What's up, gang?"

Mary Ann, a brown-haired student, excitedly explained. "Professor Cramer, Jimmy just fainted." She pointed to a student lying in a heap on the floor.

Cramer rushed over, and felt for the pulse on the student's neck. There was no discernible pulse. Cramer next put his right hand on Jimmy's forehead. His head was cold. His skin had a bluish-gray cast— probably due to lack of oxygen. Jimmy appeared to be about twenty-five years of age.

"Has anyone called for an ambulance?" Cramer asked sharply. No one spoke. Several shook their heads.

Cramer turned to the nearest student and commanded, "Go call an ambulance!"

As the student ran out of the classroom, Mary Ann pointed to another student, and said, "When Dewayne and Jimmy went to the front to put on a transparency, there was some white powder on the glass. Dewayne blew the powder off, and it got on Jimmy. Then Jimmy fell down."

At those words, Cramer remembered the computer warning— Lenny Cramer, quit the audit or your next lecture will be your last. He always used the overhead projector in his lectures. Someone had tried to kill him. One of his students was probably dead instead.

Slam had received a warning also. What was it? Something about his turning on his computer. Would the culprit put the powder on Slam's computer? I've got to call him!

Cramer turned to Mary Ann. "I have to call someone immediately. Get everyone outside now." And Cramer emphasized the word "now." "Do not let anyone get the white powder on them. Mary Ann, you wait outside the door and tell the paramedics about the white powder." The students began leaving the room. They were visibly shaken.

"Do you think it's cocaine?" Mary Ann asked.

"I doubt it," Cramer replied as he rushed out of the classroom. He ran down the hall, up one flight of stairs to his office. He dialed Slam's telephone number at Coke. After about thirty rings, there was no answer. Where was Slam? He called Slam's apartment. No answer. He tried Slam's office again.

Cramer had left his door open and he could read the brochure on the door of the tax professor across the hall:

ONLY AN ACCOUNTANT COULD CATCH AL CAPONE

Infamous mobster Al Capone wasn't easy to catch. But when Special Agents of the IRS stepped in and charged him with tax evasion, this crime czar's career came to an end. Proof that sometimes only the accountant can apprehend the criminal.

BE AN ACCOUNTANT WITH CONVICTION

It was an advertisement for an IRS Special Agent. Why couldn't he catch this madman. There was no answer at Slam's office.

Once he returned to his classroom, all of his students had left except Mary Ann. And of course, Jimmy McFeely. What a way for his students to get a walk.

The two paramedics told Cramer that the student was dead, and the coroner had been called. An autopsy would be done. Cramer shuddered as he considered the full impact of this needless tragedy. He felt nauseated.

After Cramer told the paramedics about the white powder, he hurried to his car to drive to One Coke Plaza. He had to warn Slam. He might be working late tonight.

*   *   *

Slam had heard the ringing of his office phone. It was loud. But he was staring at the white ceiling, while lying on the floor in his office. He could not move his arms and legs. He could not sit up. He could not speak or breathe. But he could think.

When he came into his office ten minutes ago, he immediately saw something that looked like baby powder on his computer. He had first thought that the building custodians had tried cleaning his equipment. But then he recalled the warnings he and Lenny had received. Perhaps someone was trying to sabotage his computer.

He remembered taking his handkerchief and carefully wiping off the computer. After dusting most of the white powder from the keyboard, he flipped on his computer. When he made his first entry, a message flashed on the screen:

SLAM, YOU ARE NOW DEAD!

"Sure I am," Slam said. He felt faint, however. He moved his chair back from the computer, tried to stand up to get some aspirins, and fell backwards. His arms and legs were numb. That was about five minutes ago. The phone was ringing again. "Someone turn it off, please."

A person rushed into his office to pick up the phone. "Why don't you wake up and answer the phone, Slam? Hmmm, nobody there now."

Slam could see he was being shaken. "Wake up, Slam! Wake up!" spoke Laura Lee.

Slam could see Laura, but he could not speak or move. He could not feel Laura's hands shaking him.

Laura walked back to his phone, dialed, and then said, "There has been an accident. Please call an ambulance and have the medics come to Room 423. Slam Duncan is sick."

Slam heard Laura leave the room, but she returned shortly with a co-worker. He could hear them whispering—as if he was dead. "I'm not dead. I just can't *move*. Help me, please."

Soon two medics rushed into the room with a stretcher. The larger medic said, "What happened?"

"I came into Slam's office to answer his phone and found him on the floor. I don't know what happened."

The second medic bent over Slam and felt his throat.

"There's no pulse." Then the medic tore open Slam's shirt and listened for Slam's heartbeat. "Did anyone here try CPR?" When no one answered, the medic frowned. "Well, it's too late now. He's dead. He must have had a heart attack. You'll need to call the coroner."

"Can't you take the body?" Laura pleaded.

"Nope. The coroner will have to declare him dead. You'll need an autopsy."

Everyone left. Slam tried to scream. He could not move. Soon he heard someone running down the hall into his office. "Slam. Oh, no. They've killed you too."

Cramer put his hand on Slam's forehead. "It's cold like the student. Where is the powder?" Cramer walked slowly around the office, stopping at the computer. He carefully looked at the system. He noticed that the screen was blank, although the computer was on. Someone must have put powder on the keyboard. Cramer sat down in a chair and waited. "I should have reported the threat." He dropped his head, feeling much remorse.

Shortly Cramer stood up, took out his handkerchief, picked up the phone, and dialed the police. "Hello. This is Lenny Cramer, in Room 423 in the Coke Building. I wish to report two murders."

"Yes. Lenny Cramer. Room 423. Coke Building. I'll wait for you."

After the phone call, Cramer found an envelope and carefully brushed some of the white powder he noticed under the computer into the envelope. He then waited.

When the police officers arrived, Cramer told them about the dead student at Georgia State. He explained about the white powder on the overhead projector and the powder under the computer. He also told them about the previous threats on the computer screens. Cramer gave the officers the envelope with the powder. "I guess someone sprinkled the stuff on the computer keyboard. But be careful. It's deadly. Could you let me know what it is?"

"You'll remain in town, Dr. Cramer? Right?"

As they finished speaking, Laura Lee walked into the room, followed by the two paramedics and a man from the coroner's office. "Hello," she croaked to Cramer. She looked pale.

★   ★   ★

Slam was finally able to move in the morgue *before* the autopsy. But he had to remain in the hospital for three days.

The poison was tetrodotoxin, one thousand times more toxic than cyanide. This highly toxic poison is found in the reproductive organs and liver of the puffer fish found off the coasts of Japan.

The powder also contained bufotenine and bufotoxin, two ingredients from dried toad skins from Haiti. The frog skin ingredients enhanced the effect of the basic poison. Voodoo powder killed one student and almost killed Slam. He was lucky. He had been a zombie for *only* four hours.

Laura Lee and Lenny visited Slam each evening in the hospital. Cramer explained in detail the incident in his classroom. "My student died from the zombie poison. Do you think Don Ball is involved. Dan Mays?" Who else might be doing this madness? The trio had no firm answer, but they made a pact to find the killer quickly.

Soon after arriving at work that morning the phone rang on Cramer's desk. He pressed the speaker-phone button. "Hello, this is Lenny Cramer."

"Lenny, I've been waiting for you to give me a call. Of course, I'd like to get together. Would you like to meet for lunch today?"

Cramer immediately recognized the voice of Will Posey. Feeling worn-out from yesterday's disaster, Cramer was tempted to put off the lunch get-together. However, he also felt a need to confide in someone. "Will, I had intended to have you over to my house ever since that nice dinner Emma prepared for Becc and me. A lot of things have kept me from getting my act together, but I'd sure like to meet for lunch. What about Ling-Po's Chinese Restaurant?"

"Great. Can you meet me there a little before noon, say 11:45? That way we can beat the main lunch crowd."

Cramer glanced at his desk calendar to be sure he could. "Sure, see you then."

"Very good. I'm looking forward to it. See ya." Then there was a click as Will hung up. Cramer turned off the speaker phone as the dial tone began.

Cramer decided to start a new area of the operational audit before leaving for lunch. He logged onto the mainframe from his personal computer. He pulled up the sales files. First he looked at the monthly sales summary reports. These were broken down by domestic and foreign sales. He pulled up the foreign reports which were further categorized by individual countries. He briefly examined each country's sales summary.

The sales summary report contained the following information. First, the title of the report and time period covered appeared at the top. This information was followed by columnar headings: location, last month's sales, current month's sales, percent change, year-to-date sales, last year's year-to-date sales, and percent change. The location column listed various city locations throughout the given country. Significant percent changes, monthly or year-to-date, were marked by asterisks on the report. A separate attached report provided explanations or comments regarding these significant changes. For example, one comment was "increase in sales due to onset of tourist season."

After reviewing the most recent month's sales summaries for a number of foreign countries, Cramer noticed it was time to leave for lunch. He logged off, picked up his coat, and left his office. The restaurant was a long walk from the Coke building, but he needed the exercise. He had just enough time to walk and make it to Ling-Po's by a quarter til noon. He set a fast pace weaving in and out of the lunch crowd.

As he entered the eating establishment he caught sight of Will sitting at a booth near the door. He glanced at his watch. The time was 11:50. Drat, he thought. He really hated being even a little late.

Will saw Lenny make his way to the booth. Both smiled wide. "Howdy, Len. You're looking good. Well, as good as a professor can look to someone who didn't like tests."

"Well, you look as good as a former IRS agent can to a disgruntled taxpayer."

"Gimme a break, Lenny. Don't tell me you're one of those nuts with a bumper sticker that says 'Stop Organized Crime, Abolish The IRS?'"

Lenny laughed. "Of course not, old friend. I'm well aware that it's the U.S. Congress that passes the tax laws. The IRS is just the collection agency. Why, I just didn't realize how sensitive you were after all those years of working for the IRS."

Will managed a weak grin. "Yeah. I reckon I've gotten more sensitive as the years have rolled by. Even though I work for Coke now and not the IRS, I'm sick and tired of people getting mad at the IRS and not their congressman. It's the people who keep electing tax-crazy politicians who make me the maddest. Well, you've gotten me off on a soapbox, and we haven't even ordered lunch yet!"

Lenny laughed again. "You always were one for soapboxes. You were out to change the world when we first met. I guess you still are."

"We've come a long way, Len. The world really has changed if you're referring to civil rights. Unfortunately we still have a ways to go, if you're talking about accounting. Well, it's really incredible how much has changed— tax laws and GAAP. The country is lawsuit-crazy and some accountants can't afford professional liability insurance. Of course, an ivory tower professor like yourself is probably unaware of these events." Will finished his comment with a chuckle. He always enjoyed kidding a friend, especially an old one like Lenny.

"Now, that's plain unfair. I'm not going to dignify that statement with a reply. Instead I'm changing the subject. How's the family? Everything seemed great the night we had dinner at your place."

"I'm happy to say that everything is going fine. Not much has changed since your visit. Emma is well. She really likes her job as a market researcher. The two girls are all grown up. They were both visiting friends the night you were over. I think I told you that Meredith is in high school and Katrina is attending Emory. She's an accounting major, of all things."

"Did her dear old dad influence her choice of major?"

"Not really. I suppose she was affected by my work. You know I really do like our field. There are a lot of options for an accounting graduate—public accounting, management accounting, and government jobs. I think she'll be happy in any one of those career paths."

They stopped talking to place their orders when the waiter came to their booth.

Will continued. "How do you like Atlanta? Has it been hard as a single parent?" Will paused. "That's a dumb question isn't it?"

"Well, we've managed fine. Sure, there have been some tough moments. Becc has adjusted well, though. I'm thankful for that. My consulting business is back in gear, thanks to your help at Coke. However, this operational audit at Coke is turning into my roughest job so far."

Cramer proceeded to tell Will about the near-murder of Slam and the tragic murder of the student. During this dialogue, the waiter brought their food.

"Man, that's some story, Lenny," Will commented as he reached for the soy sauce. "We ran into some wackos occasionally during my IRS audit days, but not murderers. Are you sure you want to continue this thing? There are other audits out there. Most of them are probably a lot less dangerous."

"No, I can't quit. This guy has got to pay. I intend to find out who he is. With Slam's help, plus your Coke colleague, Laura Lee Bertone, I figure it's just a matter of time before we find him."

Will nodded his head. "Could be a woman, equal opportunity, you know. You always were a determined fellow, Lenny." Will grinned.

The two men talked for another half an hour. When they finished, the waiter brought the check and two fortune cookies to the table.

"Well, look at this," Will stated as he read his fortune.

"It says 'Help, I'm being held prisoner in a Chinese fortune cookie factory.'" He laughed at his own joke.

"Funny," commented Cramer. "Mine says 'Beware of former IRS agents who eat at Chinese restaurants.'" Both men chuckled.

"Will, I have really enjoyed this lunch get-together. It really helped me to unload my recent disasters to a sympathetic ear. Becc and I would like to have you and your family over for dinner."

"Dinner sounds great. I'll check with Emma and get back to you, and you keep me posted on this murder investigation." The waiter walked over to pick up the check and payment. Both men reached for their wallets. "No way. I invited you for lunch, remember?"

Will replied, "Well, thanks old buddy. I guess you did."

Cramer used his American Express card. "Don't leave home without it." He gave Will a comical look. "TV commercials are brain-washing us."

After the waiter returned the card and invoice, Cramer filled in the tip and total. As they stood to leave, Will asked, "Do you want to walk back together?"

"Sure. I would have walked over with you, but I wasn't sure if I would be at Coke building this morning. As it turns out, I came from there."

"No harm done. I left early to run a few errands downtown before our rendezvous here anyway."

The two men left the restaurant together, returned to the Coke complex, and split up inside the building.

After returning to work, Cramer discovered an old newspaper clipping in one of his desk drawers. The former occupant had apparently clipped an article from a newspaper and left it in the desk. Out of curiosity, Cramer picked it up and began reading. The article described Coke's Super Bowl XXIII halftime show. Coca Cola had arranged a 3-D commercial and half-time show.

The company had packaged the 3-D glasses with Coke products. A great deal of publicity had been given to Coke regarding the first live 3-D show and commercial in network history. Cramer recalled the January 1989 Super Bowl. It had been one of the best Super Bowls ever. San Francisco beat Cincinnati with a last minute touchdown pass by Joe Montana. Paul Harvey had even described the winning play in his daily radio show, "The Rest of the Story." It turned out that the players had gotten mixed up and run the winning play wrong. Cramer thought how funny that goof-ups can sometimes work out for the best.

Cramer then returned to his examination of the Sales Summary Reports. He noticed that Coke had operations in a number of countries in Eastern Europe. He recalled that Slam and Laura were planning a trip to Poland together. Laura wanted to establish a Coke plant there, and Slam had arranged to accompany her on the trip to meet with some of the government officials. Since Slam's near-death incident, he had really hit it off with Laura. Cramer thought there was nothing wrong with that; he sometimes wished there was more romance in his own life. However, he felt he needed more time to adjust to his wife's death.

As he looked at the reports on his PC, he continued his earlier procedure to scan the "percent change" columns for the monthly sales changes and year-to-date sales changes. The significant percent changes were marked with asterisks. A separate attached report provided comments and explanations for these significant items. On one of these "comment" reports he saw a comment for the year-to-date change that he had not seen before—"same as last month." Since he had not read a "same as last month" explanation before, the oddity of it made him curious. Consequently, he pulled up the preceding month's report to see what had occurred at that time to cause a significant change in the year-to-date sales.

"Now this is getting interesting," said Cramer to himself as he looked at the prior month's sales report. On that report, as for the current month's report, there was no significant change from the prior month's sales, but the year-to-date sales were down by 70 percent from the prior year's year-to-date. And again, there was that explanation—"same as last month." Cramer pulled up the preceding month and again found the same explanation. He wondered, "How far back am I going to have to go to get an explanation other than 'same as last month?'" He pulled up the next prior month's report; that is, three months back from the current month's report, and found the same comment in both the monthly change and year-to-date change columns—"New machines. Not working properly."

Cramer realized his knowledge of Coca-Cola's dispensing machinery was rather limited, but that explanation just made him all the more curious. He began wondering what else could explain the unusual change. "How could new machines cause a drop-off in the month's sales four months in a row? If there was a problem, it should have been fixed before now. However, it was in an Eastern European country. Perhaps, some local government official was actually causing the problem. Or perhaps, the local help was slow to fix an American firm's equipment." He made a note in his workpapers to investigate further, when his phone rang.

"I've got something," Slam Duncan said quietly into the receiver. Cramer, on the other end responded. "I'll come down to your work center."

"No," Duncan retorted. "I'll come up to your office. It's in a quieter section of the building. More secure. This is big! I think I know whodunit."

"Well, don't delay! Get up here and tell me."

CHAPTER 11

The great composer does not set to work because he is inspired, but becomes inspired because he is working. Beethoven, Wagner, Bach, and Mozart settled down day after day to the job in hand with as much regularity as an accountant settles down each day to his figures. They didn't waste time for an inspiration.

— Ernest Newman

"Don't you get it, Lenny? This guy has to be our man. He's been retired for a few years, and he's beginning to feel pinched living on his fixed retirement income. Then, presto-whammo, he gets an idea—steal some valuable information from my old employer and sell it to a rival company."

"Whoa, buddy. I understand Doyle Loebbecke was in charge of programming when Coke installed their last system, but please explain again why you think he's the hacker."

"Ok. First of all, he's the only one with sufficient knowledge of the system to be able to do it. We know the hacker used a Trojan-Horse type of trap door to get into the system. Only a programmer with intimate knowledge of the system could do that. But to move around in the system would require more than just the getting-in kind of knowledge. It requires knowledge of additional passwords, and more importantly, how the system is configured. This guy would know that. But here's the clincher—he's using the same account number he had twenty years ago. I went back through the old master lists of valid user-IDs and related passwords since Coke got their first dial-in computer system. His old ID and password were there and match the ones the hacker used."

"Slam, gimme a break. He couldn't be that stupid. Why would he use a number that's bound to give him away?"

"I thought about that. Two reasons. One, it's twenty-years old. Who'd think to look through the old records except a genius like myself. Two, he's desperate and couldn't break into the system any other way. Also, we still can't prove he stole anything of value yet. All he has done is retrieve tons of inventory records data, primarily about shipments received. But here's where it gets interesting. I have a theory. Don't laugh."

Cramer smiled a crooked smile. "Laugh. I can't laugh. I can't wait for you to make sense of all this for me."

"The Coke formula. He's after the Coke formula!"

The two men stared at each other for a few moments.

Cramer burst out laughing. "You're kidding me. Water, sugar, carbon dioxide, and the Seven X." He kept laughing.

Duncan just stared at Cramer. "Would you stop that. Don't you see, he's after the Seven X part of the formula. Listen to me."

Tears rolled down Cramer's cheeks. He couldn't stop laughing, although he was laughing less hard now. He knew that carbon dioxide gave coke its fizziness, and the color of coke came from caramel.

Duncan continued, "The inventory records are the key. Doyle Loebbecke worked for Coke for almost forty years. Don't you think he was aware of opportunities for industrial spying. This soft drink business is super-competitive. It's a war out there. Sure, Coke is number one, but they have some mean competitors, especially Pepsi. You've heard of the 'Pepsi Challenge' haven't you?"

Cramer had managed to quit laughing. He wiped the tears of laughter from his eyes. "You're serious, aren't you?" he asked.

"Dead serious. I think this is the guy who tried to kill me."

Cramer was taken aback by that statement. "All right. Let's assume you're right, just for the sake of discussion. How does he get the Coke formula from the inventory records? The formula is one of the most highly guarded corporate secrets in the world of corporate secrets. I reckon the Colonel's secret recipe of 11 herbs and spices is the only thing close in terms of major corporate secrets."

"Thanks for hearing me out," Duncan responded with a bit of indignation. He was a bit miffed from Cramer's unnecessary laughter. "I didn't understand the significance of the inventory records at first myself, but as I pondered over it day and night, it finally occurred to me. Loebbecke is analyzing the records to derive the Coke formula."

"How?" Cramer asked.

"By accumulating years and years of records, and by being intimately aware of Coke's production cycles, Loebbecke can determine exactly what combination of ingredients is necessary to make the world's most popular soft drink. He can then sell the formula to the highest bidder in the industry."

"Pepsi?" Cramer responded.

"Perhaps. Or some newcomer to the soft drink field. Maybe to a foreign country. India. China. Remember India kicked Coke out a number of years ago. They have a similar cola, but it doesn't taste as good. Once in a while a new brand pops up. Most only last a few years. Rarely do any make a profit. People know Coke, and they just keep coming back to it after trying the no-names for a while."

"Well, you have me interested, Slam. India. It's quite a theory, barely plausible. If all you say is true, why did Loebbecke unleash the virus into the system?"

"Elementary, my dear professor. Loebbecke found out about our audit, and he decided to cover his tracks. Did you know that the Coke system staff could not find back-ups to some of the destroyed files. Fortunately, yours truly had downloaded some of the crucial ones back at the beginning of our audit job, such as the old master lists of user-IDs and passwords I just mentioned."

"But what made him so desperate that he tried to kill us?" Cramer interrupted.

"I suppose he thought we were going to stop his money-making plans from coming to fruition. Maybe he thought our operational audit was aimed specifically at him. Maybe he just didn't like our looks. Maybe he doesn't like my mustache. But I have a plan to get some hard evidence to prove he's the hacker."

"Well, go on, don't leave me hanging."

Duncan continued. "First, we arrange to have the phone lines monitored. Next time he logs on, we will have the call traced to his house. That's the main strategy. But being the resourceful guy that I am, I also have a back-up plan. I have the guy's address, and I'm gonna tap into his computer system."

"Tap in? You think he has a dial-in service on his PC?"

"I doubt it. But that's not how I'm getting into his castle." Slam lowered his voice to a whisper. "I purchased some electronic eavesdropping equipment, my friend. The stuff cost me $500. You'll see it on my next expense report. The equipment consists of a battery-powered TV set, a TV antenna, and some basic electronic gear. Primarily a couple of oscillators."

"You're beginning to sound like James Bond. How does this spy stuff work?"

"Well, I plan to park in front of Loebbecke's house and tune into his PC's display screen. Most computer systems emanate electromagnetic radiation from the circuitry and from their CRTs. The CRT—uh, that is, cathode-ray tube—is what shoots the beam of electrons that form the image on the monitor screen. My spy gear will allow me to tune into that signal. If all goes as planned, I'll be able to see exactly what Loebbecke sees on his screen. Also, I plan to record it on a portable VCR to further prove his guilt."

Duncan paused in his monologue for Cramer's reaction. Cramer didn't say anything immediately and Duncan continued. "By the way, I'll need to rent a van to work from. My bike isn't big enough to hold all this gear, let alone to do my work secretly, if you know what I mean?"

Cramer began slowly smiling and shaking his head. "This audit is really getting crazy." He began humming the theme from the classic TV series, "The Twilight Zone." Duncan joined in. They both laughed.

After discussing some practical details to the spy caper, Cramer and Duncan said goodbye. Cramer meant to discuss the unusual sales summary report from the Polish location with Duncan but forgot to bring it up during all of Duncan's revelations regarding the former Coke executive. Well, he'd try to remember to tell Duncan about it before he went overseas with Laura Lee.

Cramer looked at his watch. "Good grief," he thought, "I need to look over my notes on expert systems before driving over to the campus."

★   ★   ★

As Cramer entered the classroom, he knew it would be difficult to have a normal lecture so soon after Jimmy McFeely's tragic death. What really grieved Cramer was the fact that Jimmy McFeely had died as a result of the misfortune of being in Dr. Lenny Cramer's auditing class. None of the other auditing professors had provoked any homicidal maniacs.

Cramer could not bring back the dead student, but he would not rest until he found the student's killer. Cramer noticed on his class roster that Dewayne had dropped the class. Poor Dewayne would always feel guilty that he had been the one to blow the voodoo powder off the overhead projector and onto Jimmy. Cramer decided that he would try to have a visit with Dewayne. After all, if anyone was to blame, Cramer thought, it wasn't Dewayne but Cramer himself.

He placed an overhead transparency on the projector with some hesitancy, momentarily recalling it was one of the murderer's tools. He pointed to the screen and said, "Today we will look at a fascinating new tool available to the auditor. Expert systems have been developed for a number of auditing applications."

"You've probably heard of artificial intelligence or AI. Expert systems are an extension of this field. Many areas of accounting practice are being affected by artificial intelligence, specifically, through the use of expert systems applications. Areas affected include management accounting, auditing, consulting, and tax practice."

"Artificial intelligence is concerned with making computers behave in ways that would be considered intelligent in a human being. With AI, and expert systems in particular, the accounting field will experience changes in the way that managers and staff interact and use the computer resources of the organization."

A student raised her hand. "Yes," Cramer responded, nodding his head toward Sonya Thornhill.

"Professor Cramer, do you think there will be a reduction in the number of accountants because of these expert systems, and because of computers in general?"

Cramer was a little miffed by Sonya's interruption, particularly since the question was changing the primary direction of his lecture. He had to get out of this foul mood.

"In a way, yes," replied Cramer. "However, there will be plenty of job opportunities in the foreseeable future. No one is predicting a decrease in accounting jobs. True, the computer has enabled accountants to do their jobs more efficiently. And by reducing the time required to do an audit, for example, a CPA firm can do the audit using fewer staff. Logically the firm could then trim its staff size. But most firms are expanding in size. That's because firms are offering more types of services than in the past."

"Should I back up and discuss how computers have generally affected the accounting field?" asked Cramer. Several students nodded their heads.

"The computer has had an impact on the accounting field in three distinct phases. The first phase was automated record keeping and transaction processing. The second phase included development of computerized accounting information systems and on-line interactive information processing. Both of these phases affected human behavior and changed the way accounting was performed within organizations. The third phase includes advanced decision support and expert systems. This third phase promises to have the most pronounced effect on accounting and other business-related activities."

Lenny began to slowly pace across the front of the class. "As computer hardware and support software developed, it became possible to integrate all of the accounting applications and other functional areas within the organization. Through the use of data base management systems, that is, DBMS, the manager could access and request information from the computer interactively."

"This led the way for the development of formalized managerial reporting and display systems—the computerized management information system or MIS. The accounting information system, that is, AIS, is a subsystem of the MIS. The AIS provides management with the financial-oriented decision making information."

"The current phase of computer applications for the accounting field centers on the workstation concept. For the accountant the workstation can be a stand-alone unit or device connected to the corporate system. The workstation consists of a microcomputer or intelligent terminal which has local or personal data storage, local printing and report output presentation facilities."

"The accounting function will utilize a wide range of software tools as the workstation comes into use. Many of the functions and face-to-face interactions will be altered. The personal computer tools for the electronic desk include the following: word processing and memo writing; spreadsheet and business graphics; data management; and communications. Communication changes will affect accounting, not only in mainframe to micro communication, but in electronic mail, messaging, and even electronic fund transferring."

Cramer looked around the room. Several students were nodding off. He realized his lecture might be a little stale. He thought of a joke he heard at a past meeting of the American Accounting Association. The luncheon speaker told the attendees, mostly professors, that he once dreamed he was lecturing. He woke up and he was. Cramer chuckled and continued lecturing.

"Software tools, such as statistical and management science packages, application development packages, and report generators are changing the quality of data analysis, the speed and personalization of application development, and the presentation of information. However, the latest tool set, decision support and expert systems, will force the accountants and their staff to re-think and even modify their approach to the accounting process."

"Donald Waterman defined expert systems as 'sophisticated computer programs that manipulate knowledge to solve problems efficiently and effectively in a narrow problem domain.'" Cramer stopped his lecture to place an overhead transparency on the projector.

The image on screen showed the following:

1. An explicit and accessible body of knowledge, known as the knowledge base. This includes the rules and facts applicable to a particular domain—a domain being a range of acceptable values; and

2. An inference engine which allows the application of the rules and facts in the knowledge base to a problem.

Cramer pointed to the screen and said, "These are the two basic components of an expert system. These two components are combined to give 'true' expert systems four fundamental characteristics." Cramer paused and replaced the overhead transparency with one showing the following:

1. Expertise—an expert system should exhibit expert performance, have a high level of skill (efficient and effective) and have adequate robustness (depth and breadth in a subject).

2. Symbolic Reasoning—it should represent knowledge symbolically (not mathematically) and be able to reformulate arbitrary symbolic knowledge with which it can work.

3. Depth—an expert system should be able to operate effectively in a narrow domain containing difficult, challenging problems.

4. Self-knowledge—it should be able to examine its own reasoning and apply rules to check the accuracy, consistency, and plausibility of its conclusions. An expert system should also be able to explain its reasoning.

"Thus, an expert system attempts to solve problems like an expert in a particular domain. Just like all experts, they produce correct answers most of the time and incorrect answers some of the time."

"Dr. Cramer," a student interrupted without raising his hand. "Is an expert system a type of decision support system?"

"Not exactly, Mark," Cramer replied. "A decision support system, that is, a DSS is exactly what the name says. A DSS supports the decision-making by a human but does not make the decision. An expert system, on the other hand, attempts to make a decision in a particular domain. Thus, a human is essential in the use of a DSS, while a 'true' expert system does not need one to reach a decision."

"Most users of expert systems attempt to keep a human in the loop due to the fact that human expertise is currently much better in certain areas. Humans are more creative and can learn in difficult domains. Additionally, they can see the big picture, and probably most importantly, they have common sense. Therefore, in a way, expert systems are like decision support systems in most domains since they act as a consultant to the human."

"There are quite a few ways to build expert systems, but they all can be thought of as having two principal components: a knowledge base and an inference engine. These components are designed to allow us to represent knowledge about some portion of the real world — usually quite a small portion — and then to give the computer a method for reasoning within the body of knowledge so it can solve problems."

"The knowledge base in the most common form of expert system, which is known as a rule-based system, consists of a series of if/then rules concerning pertinent objects and events." Cramer wrote "if/then" on the overhead. "The 'if' part of the rule presents the situation. The 'then' part is the response. For example, in an expert system for financial statement analysis, if evidence indicates liquidity deterioration, then the response is that liquidity status needs improvement."

"Such rules, which are known as the system's heuristics, can be added or subtracted from, as the program is used. This flexibility is one of the advantages of expert systems—from the moment an accounting staff member has encoded more than a few rules, he or she has set up a working system that can be constantly refined as more rules are added. A true expert system typically needs at least twenty rules to be a valid mirror of the subject it covers, while some may have more than a thousand. Most systems have well over one hundred rules."

"Another type of expert system is the example-based system. In place of rules, these systems have recorded examples, such as: 'bad ratios and slow turnovers denote liquidity deterioration.' When enough of these rules have been entered into the knowledge base, the system can induce a rule which is then stated in an if/then construction."

"However, rules or examples are not enough—these alone comprise nothing more than a data base. *Now write this down.* What makes an expert system expert is the way the rules are processed by the system and how they are acted upon— this is done by the inference engine." He repeated the sentence.

"The two most common inference methods are *backward* chaining or goal driven, and *forward* chaining or data driven. Think about the *Texas Chainsaw Massacre* movie. As the name implies, backward chaining starts with the 'then' part of an if/then statement—a goal or result—and when this matches the same component in a problem, the system searches for appropriate 'if' clause. Forward chaining works in reverse order."

"Whether the system uses forward chaining, backward chaining or a combination of the two, several 'if' or 'then' clauses may be true at the same time. The system has to weigh these, deciding which is more important or meaningful in a given problem; and then show the user how the decision was reached. In most expert systems a combination of techniques is employed."

"The most important part of an expert system is the analysis of how experts come to conclusions and the determination of which kinds and sets of facts are the most useful in the process."

Cramer stopped for a moment and then continued.

"The development of accounting expert systems is just beginning. Accounting expert systems are being developed in the three broad accounting fields of auditing, taxation, and management accounting. Accounting expert systems apply to specific accounting-related problems; such as evaluating internal controls, analyzing a firm's allowance for bad debts, auditing advanced EDP systems, and evaluating tax-related problems."

"Accounting expert systems not only impact the accounting profession in solving accounting problems but also will aid in the recruitment, education, and development of personnel. Expert systems can assist in training and educating new accountants. Since the accounting neophytes can be taught the rules and reasoning that an expert in the field actually uses, the quality of training that a new employee receives should improve."

"The first expert system, that is ES, in auditing dealt with the auditor's evaluation of a commercial client's Allowance for Bad Debts. Two accounting researchers, Hansen and Messier, subsequently began an investigation of EDP control evaluation employing the ES approach. Another type of ES analysis, called TICOM, was developed by Bailey,

Duke, Gerlach, Ko, Merservy, and Whinston. TICOM, which stands for 'The Internal Control Monitor', does an analysis of the flow of documents and effectiveness of controls, recommends additional controls and points out potential weaknesses. An auditor using TICOM would first complete a traditional review of the internal control system and then, if an extensive evaluation were desired, employ TICOM to model the system. TICOM is superior to traditional internal control evaluation methods in the following ways: one, the evaluation can be more exhaustive; two, the documentation of the system can be more thorough; and three, the modeler/auditor may probe and test controls by using the query-processing portion of TICOM."

"Other auditing research projects in the ES area include two Ph.D. dissertations at Michigan State University, Steinbart, 1984, and Gal, 1985. Theoretical usefulness of expert systems has been demonstrated, and practical applications are currently being tested. One example of a practical project was a study by Willingham and Wright with assistance from a major accounting firm, in which an expert system was developed to assist in the audit of bank loan collectibility. A goal of this project was to have the system available for use by the firm's auditors in the field."

"Research has demonstrated the usefulness of ES to auditing. ES can be used for planning the audit program, analytic review, internal control evaluation, continuous auditing, and system design."

"There are numerous potential applications of ES. It is anticipated that the codification of Statements on Auditing Standards will serve as a knowledge base for an auditing expert system in the near future. This auditing standards-based expert system may involve the use of one of the newer artificial intelligence software systems, such as PROLOG or LISP."

"Many future ES applications will be written by the users themselves. General purpose expert systems are being developed which enable people in various fields, such as business, engineering, medical diagnosis, and others, to create their own expert system applications."

Cramer stopped lecturing when he noticed several students were apparently asleep. Their eyes were open, but there seemed to be no mental activity occurring behind them. He knew this condition meant it was time to ask a few questions.

"Mark," Cramer called to the student who interrupted his lecture earlier. "Would you like to use an auditing expert system?"

"It would probably help on test days," Mark replied. Laughter slowly erupted from the class. Cramer smiled. He was glad to see everyone perk up.

After the laughter stopped, Mark continued, "Seriously, Dr. Cramer, I'm not too sure I want to work with a machine that's smarter than me. The machine might start telling me what to do!"

There was more laughter.

"A lot of people have the same basic concern, Mark, but I don't think you have to worry about a machine being truly smarter than you. Machines will never have true human intelligence; that's why we call it 'artificial' intelligence. They'll never take over the world—except in the movies."

"Overcoming people's reluctance to work with computers is an important area of research. Designing a useful computer-based information system requires more than just technical knowledge. Sensitivity to human needs and behavior is as important a component as specialized technical knowledge. Involving people in the systems development process is critical to the ultimate success of any system, including an expert system."

"In an article in *Psychology Today*, Neil Frude states the following. I quote. 'The ideal companion machine would not only look, feel and sound friendly but would also be programmed to behave in a congenial manner. Those qualities which make interaction with other people enjoyable would be simulated as closely as possible, and the machine would appear to be charming, stimulating, and easygoing.... It can be anticipated that computer systems will be future friends and intimates as well as colleagues.' End of quote."

"Expert systems in business may be the first step in unlocking the computer's potential as described by Frude. If the computer can be programmed to emulate the decision-making abilities of an 'expert,' then *perhaps* the computer can also be programmed to behave in a congenial manner. People would then enjoy interacting with this super user-friendly 'expert' who was also personable and easy-going."

"The development of the computer and, more recently, the proliferation of microcomputers are having a tremendous impact on the way businesses operate. Developments in expert systems may ultimately yield the single greatest impact on business operations. An 'expert's' opinion would be as available as one's desk-top computer."

"Well, I see we're nearly out of time. Does anyone have any questions or comments about expert systems?"

Cramer waited a moment. No one responded to his question. He then asked, "Has anyone read anything about auditing recently? In the newspaper or a professional journal?"

Everyone started stacking their books, anxious to leave the classroom. Suddenly there was a murmur of discontent as Jeff Miller raised his hand. Cramer motioned for Jeff to ask his question.

"Dr. Cramer, I saw an article in last month's *Journal of Accountancy* that referred to the expectations gap. What's that?" The question was asked by one of Cramer's favorite students. Jeff seemed genuinely interested in learning.

"Jeff, that is a real troublesome issue to the profession. The problem relates to the misunderstanding or misperception by the general public regarding the auditor's role in an audit."

"I get it," Jeff interrupted. "The public expects something different from what the auditor actually does."

"Exactly," Cramer responded. Cramer smiled. He had already prepared some lecture notes on this topic. He pulled out some pages from among his voluminous lecture notes and began reading.

"The general counsel of one Big Six firm described the misperception problem several years ago. He stated that misconceptions in the public mind are at least fivefold. The *first* area relates to scope—that auditors make a 100% examination of the company's records, which can be depended upon to uncover all errors or misconduct. The *second* area relates to evaluation—that auditors evaluate the wisdom and legality of a company's multitudinous business decisions. The *third* area concerns precision—that the numbers set forth in a company's audited financial statements are immutable absolutes. The *fourth* area relates to reducibility—that the audited results of a company's operations for a year can be synthesized into a single number. The *fifth* area concerns approval—that by expressing an opinion on a company's financial statement, the auditors 'certify' its health and attractiveness for investment purposes."

Cramer paused a minute while his students briskly wrote notes on his remarks. When most students stopped writing, he began again.

"The public must understand that an accountant differs from a product manufacturer in several important respects. An auditor does not have absolute control over a company's finances and records in the same way that a product manufacturer has knowledge of and control over production processes. The relationship between the auditor and the client's financial statements, which are the responsibility of man-

119

agement, is indirect; whereas the relationship between a defective product and the manufacturer is direct."

"The effect of these misconceptions culminates in the failure of the courts and juries to distinguish between an audit failure and a business failure. Although the auditor adds credibility to financial statements through an independent examination, the extent to which the auditor's report affects the judgment of investors is uncertain and speculative. In purchasing a product, a consumer expects an adequate product. In accountant's liability litigation there seems to be a failure in understanding a basic fact, that rational investors take risks hoping to reap financial profit from their investments, but nevertheless are aware of the ever-present possibility of loss."

"Recent research suggests that many financial statement users misunderstand the auditor's role and responsibilities. Users may be unaware of limitations of the audit function and may be unclear regarding the distinction between the responsibilities of management and those of the auditor. There is an ongoing effort by the profession to more clearly explain these responsibilities, and thus, to close the expectations gap."

Cramer noticed several students had started shuffling around in their desks. Jeff was the only one who appeared to be listening with any interest.

"Well, I see ya'll are ready to go. Class dismissed. *Adios*."

Everyone jumped up and headed out of the classroom. Cramer thought to himself that the whole process resembled a cattle stampede.

★   ★   ★

He thought about his daughter on the drive home. Becc wouldn't be there. She was spending the night with a new-found friend from school. Becc had made this arrangement after Cramer had been called as a witness for a Congressional hearing. He was taking a late evening flight from Hartsfield International Airport to National Airport in Washington, D.C., and would be out of town for just one night. He knew Becc was old enough to take care of herself when he was out of town, but he preferred her to stay with someone when he had to travel overnight.

He had given Becc his phone number for the Hyatt Regency in Crystal City. Crystal City is a conglomeration of hotels and shops very close to National Airport; consequently, the cab ride from airport to hotel was only about five minutes. Cramer preferred short cab rides, even when he wasn't exhausted after a flight.

After stopping by the house, he headed over to Hartsfield. The only luggage he had was his Zenith laptop computer and a hanging bag. He carried these on the plane, and the flight was uneventful. He did enjoy the bird's eye view of the nation's capital at night. Landing at National Airport was a little discomforting. The runways at this older airport were shorter than most; consequently, the large passenger jets had to brake rather hard on landing. "The airport's convenient location is well worth this small price, though," Cramer thought.

The cab ride and hotel check-in went smoothly. Before going to sleep he looked over some information about the Dingell Committee before which he was scheduled to testify in the morning. But his mind would drift to Don Ball and Doyle Loebbecke. "Were they the bad guys? Was it someone else?"

CHAPTER 12

The objectives of the auditor's review of accounting control within EDP are similar to those for manual and mechanical processing. The review is an information-gathering process that depends on knowledgeable inquiries directed to client personnel, observation of job assignments and operating procedures, and reference to available documentation related to accounting control.

— AICPA Professional Standards

"Before I introduce our next witness, let me quote from a recent article in the *Wall Street Journal* by Lee Berton." The speaker was Congressman John D. Dingell (D-Michigan), who was chairing the Subcommittee on Oversight of Investigations of the House Energy and Commerce Committee.

"Mr. Berton indicates that many investors wonder how an outside auditor can give a clean opinion to financial results that so quickly turn sour. They have long believed that a clean opinion—one not citing any severe corporate problems—is like the Good Housekeeping Seal of Approval."

Lenny Cramer was waiting to testify before Dingell's committee. He was not quite as nervous as the last time he testified here, but he knew that the colorful Dingell was preparing to hang Lenny out to dry. Oh well, that was the price of testifying before Congress.

John Dingell gestured toward Lenny behind the microphone. "We have here today Professor Leonard Cramer, a Certified Public Accountant and practitioner in Atlanta. He also teaches at Georgia State University. Dr. Cramer, why shouldn't auditors be more responsible for detecting management fraud? What disclosures should Congress force auditors to make on financial statements?"

After a short pause, Cramer said, "Thank you Chairman Dingell for this opportunity to speak to your committee today. First, let me point out the main function of a Certified Public Accountant."

Lenny paused for a moment as he looked at each of the five committee members. "A CPA's main function is to certify to the world that the financial statements *as prepared by management* fairly present the financial position, results of operations, and cash flows for the period audited. The auditor evaluates the accounting principles used and significant estimates, made by management, as well as evaluating the overall financial statement presentation."

"Professor Cramer," Representative Dingell interjected, "What about the discovery of management fraud? This committee has heard John Shank state: At the very time an auditor should be the most cynical and skeptical about a company is when his client is applying the most pressure." Dingell smiled broadly.

Cramer continued. "A clean opinion by an auditor is *not* a Good Housekeeping Seal of Approval. The financial statements are management's responsibility. Auditors can *not* absolutely guarantee that financial statements prepared by management are free from material misstatement. As a CPA myself, I can only provide *reasonable assurances* that audited financials are free from any material misstatement."

"Professors Arens and Loebbecke in their fine auditing textbook point out the dilemma quite well. Let me quote them."

Cramer began reading from a photocopy page. "The auditor cannot *serve* as the insurer or guarantor of financial statement accuracy or business health. The audit costs to society that would be required to achieve such high levels of assurance would exceed the benefits. Moreover, even with increased audit costs, well-planned frauds would not necessarily be discovered, nor errors of judgment eliminated. End of quote."

"Carl Liggio, general counsel for pre-merger Arthur Young & Company indicates that an auditor who would catch all fraud would be too expensive—perhaps four to six times the cost of current audits, which run from several thousand dollars for small companies to more than one million for major corporations. Who will pay for such perfection?"

Lenny raised his voice. "Look, auditors are not trained to detect forgeries, nor will current audit procedures detect all conspiracies. Mr. Liggio tells the story about one auditor-negligence court battle involving fraud by the owner of the company. This owner sent his personal pilot by plane to intercept confirmation requests about cash and assets that the conscientious auditor had express-mailed to suppliers and lenders. The pilot signed off on the confirmations and sent them back to the unsuspecting auditor. How can an auditor catch something like that?'"

"Just a moment, Dr. Cramer," another Representative interjected. "This committee has examined a number of auditing problems where the auditor was *not* independent. There was Penn Square Bank where partners had below market loans with the bank in excess of one million dollars. Remember Beverly Hills Savings? Here an audit partner served on the audit engagement for a number of years and allowed overstatement of assets based on appraisals by a non-independent appraiser."

The gray-haired Representative stopped for a moment and picked up a sheet of paper. "The *Wall Street Journal* quoted the audit partner-in-charge of the ESM mess concerning the pressure on auditors. I quote. 'In 1977 it became apparent to me that those being promoted early were the business producers... they were the ones that were able to produce new clients. The salesmen. It became apparent to me... that my own promotion depended on my becoming more productive. That's when I began turning more sales-oriented. I think I would have been able to be more objective about my client relationships if I weren't so concerned about selling .... If I had not had the sales pressure, I would perhaps have caught it before it happened.' End of Quote."

Lenny raised his voice, "The AICPA Professional Standards indicate that an auditor *must* retain his integrity and objectivity in all phases of their practice and, when expressing opinions on financial statements, avoid involvement in situations that would impair the credibility of their independence. Certainly when a partner takes bribes and subverts his own firm's quality procedures in order to cover prior year's audit errors—as was the case with ESM—independence has been breached."

Lenny looked at Dingell, but he was conferring with someone behind him. "Thus, please let me summarize. For several decades auditors have used such substantive tests as reconciling, tracing, and vouching in order to verify mechanical accuracy. The computer has caused these traditional procedures to become less efficient and effective."

"Ronald L. Clark at my sister institution—University of Georgia—states it very well. 'Today's auditors are increasingly using analytics to gather evidence on transactions and internal controls. Audit risk has not only increased, but the concept of how to address and control risk has changed. Computer fraud, always a problem, could rise to alarming levels due to the increased number of computer end-users, databases and communication networks.' End of quote."

"Thank you, Dr. Cramer, for your opinion about the crisis of confidence in the accounting profession." Congressman Dingell stated further, "Auditors are paid by the same hands they oversee. They are not paid to blow the whistle against their clients. May we have the next witness, Wanda A. Wallace, the Deborah D. Shelton Systems Professor at Texas A&M University."

At that point, Cramer wished he could say more, but his small contribution to this hearing had ended. He knew of Wallace's research. He thought, "No doubt she'll do a better job than me defending our honorable profession from these unwarranted attacks. Why, these Congressmen are just trying to make names for themselves by inventing scapegoats for the country's problems. Heck, if they really wanted to do something good, they'd clean up their own act and balance the budget on a regular basis."

As he left the hearing, he realized he had a few hours to kill before he had to return to the Hyatt. "Great, I'll walk the Mall." He walked briskly from the Capitol which was at the east end of the Mall. Cramer laughed to himself as he recalled a story about some tourists who thought that the Washington, D.C. Mall was an indoor shopping mall full of stores. In actuality the Mall is a broad expanse of open land around which the most famous national monuments are situated. He walked down the Capitol steps looking toward the Washington Monument which stood about a mile and half away in the center of the Mall. Beyond that tall monument, at the west end was the Lincoln Memorial. Close to the Lincoln Memorial was the Mall's newest addition, the Vietnam Veteran's Memorial, referred to as "The Wall."

Cramer could not resist a brief visit inside the Air and Space Museum, one of the 14 museums operated by the Smithsonian Institution. "Funny," he thought, "the Smithsonian was established by funds bequeathed to the U.S. by an Englishman, James Smithson. Little did that guy know what a famous American institution he would begin. Unlike Disneyland, admission is free."

Leaving the Air and Space Museum, Cramer continued down the sidewalk alongside Jefferson Drive, passing the Smithsonian Castle which housed the Institution's first museum. The Castle is what comes to most people's minds when they think of the Smithsonian. Today it is primarily administrative offices.

Cramer walked up the hill on which the Washington Monument stands. Flapping in the wind were the flags circling the monument. He could not help the patriotic feeling that surged through him. In some small way he hoped that he made a contribution to the country's future welfare and prosperity. After resting a few minutes, he continued his long walk along the Mall, passing the large reflecting pools, to the Lincoln Memorial. Inside the memorial, even though he had seen Lincoln's statue before, he gazed with awe. He read the words chiseled into the marble walls:

> . . . Intelligence, patriotism, Christianity, and a firm reliance on Him who has never yet forsaken this favored land are still competent to adjust in the best way all our present difficulty . . . As was said three thousand years ago, so still it must be said, 'the judgements of the Lord are true and righteous altogether.'

"What a horrible time for our country," thought Cramer. "More Americans were killed in the Civil War than all the other wars combined. The sixteenth president had resolved not to allow the southern states to secede. Lincoln, a Christian, often looked for wisdom and inspiration from the Bible. Reflecting on the prospects of a broken nation, he quoted the words of Jesus, 'A house divided against itself shall not stand.'"

From the Lincoln Memorial, Cramer walked over to the Vietnam Veteran's Memorial. "Another sad war," he thought. On an earlier trip to Washington, he had found the names of several friends and relatives lost during that bitter conflict. His eyes grew misty as he reflected on the tragic deaths of those men, literally cut down in their prime. "War is hell! General Sherman was absolutely right." Wiping his eyes, he wondered if there would be a memorial for the highly successful Iraqi war. Slowly he began his trek back to the Smithsonian Castle. There he would take the Metro, Washington's subway, to Crystal City where the Hyatt was located.

At the hotel he checked out and took the hotel's shuttle bus to National Airport. He was over an hour early for his flight. The flight was delayed and it was over two hours before he was on his way back to Atlanta. He was glad that Becc would be home to greet him.

After a cheerful reunion at home Cramer thought how fortunate he was to have a daughter. After settling into bed his mind drifted to the Coke audit. He realized he would not see Slam the next day. Slam, at the request of Posey, was accompanying Laura Bertone on an overseas trip to Poland. Cramer hoped the two of them would have a pleasant trip together. "Romance is in the air," he thought before drifting off to sleep. "Maybe I can find the smoking gun while he's gone. Don Ball? Doyle Loebbecke? Both? Someone else?"

The next morning at work, Cramer decided to ask Will Posey about Doyle Loebbecke.

"Sure I know him," Posey began. "He was the resident computer nut when I started working at Coke. But he retired not long after that."

"What do you know about him?" Cramer asked.

"Not much really. He seemed to be a very refined, older gentleman. Very friendly. I had to get his help with some programming problems a few times. Unlike some computer experts I know, Loebbecke spoke plain English, not computer jargon. He really knew his stuff. He could explain things so that anyone could understand. You know I really hate it when anyone tells me that some so-called expert knows his stuff, but just can't explain it to others. Heck, that expert doesn't know his stuff. He's just faking it!"

"Whoa, buddy. You're getting on one of your soapboxes. Let's get back to the subject. You remember, Loebbecke? Do you know what he's doing now?"

"Well, I heard that he's seeing the world. He sends a postcard back to the old gang here at Coke once in a while. We post them on the bulletin board in the coffee room. The last one is still up, some place in Pakistan. No, India, I think. He may be back home by now. Why are you so interested in Doyle? Some question about the computer system?"

"Yeah, basically that's it. I'll tell you all about it later." Cramer started leaving Posey's office.

"Hold on, Lenny. I just remembered something. When Laura Lee began work at Coke, she started in Loebbecke's department. She could probably tell you more about him."

Cramer scratched his head. "That's a big help, Will. I'll check with her when she gets back from overseas. Thanks for the info." Cramer turned and left Posey's office.

As he walked toward his office, Cramer mused over his newfound nformation. "This is great! If Loebbecke is the culprit, then Laura may be able to help us figure out exactly what he did. Meanwhile I'll get the spy equipment Slam purchased and see if I can pick up any computer signals from outside Loebbecke's home. This caper is getting too interesting to wait 'til Slam and Laura get back."

CHAPTER 13

Although the Internal Revenue Service has computer systems to support specific functions, such as collection and examination, these systems have never been integrated due to design constraints of the master file processing system. The result is that users of these systems are confronted with taxpayers account data that differ in format, content and degree of accessibility.

— GAO Report

After a short fuel break in Paris, their Pan Am 747 flight landed at Tegel Airport in Berlin. Slam Duncan and Laura Bertone collected their suitcases and rented a blue Ford. Slam had a difficult time getting Laura's large suitcases in the trunk. Soon they drove southwest toward the center of the city.

"We still have some time before dusk. I'll take you to see remnants of 'the Wall.' The best viewing spot is at Potsdamer Platz," Laura said.

Before 1989, the wall split Berlin in half. The Western half of the city was once a sealed island, surrounded by East Germany. The Wall appeared overnight on August 13, 1961, to prevent immigration from East Berlin. However, beginning in the fall of 1989, the wall was dismantled and the communist government allowed its citizens the freedom to travel. Civil unrest in East Germany and other communist countries pressured their leaders to make changes. East and West Germany were re-united in 1990. Political reform began taking place throughout Eastern Europe.

At Potsdamer Platz, Laura and Slam scrambled up a platform to look at what was once the East German zone. Pointing to a desolate spot, Laura said, "See that small mound of dirt? That's the air raid shelter where Hitler committed suicide in 1945."

"I read that at least three-and-one-half million Germans fled from the East to the West before the Wall was built in 1961. That was a big brain drain," Slam interjected. "After the wall was dismantled in 1989, some people left East Germany, but the overwhelming majority stayed in their native country with the hope that the new freedoms would remain in effect. Eventually the two countries merged."

The old wall was really two walls with a no-man's-land between the two. In the middle was the killing zone—land mines, attack dogs, and self-triggering shotguns. Occasionally, along the route, stood a watch tower with two soldiers. A bonus was paid for any person the guards stopped—dead or alive. The guards were never put on duty twice together to avoid the development of a friendship. Two friendly guards might have escaped together.

Laura laughed. "I'm impressed by the Berliners' attitude. Apparently most of the Wall was painted in this colorful graffiti."

"I agree. Let's get a picture of the Wall." Slam climbed down from the platform and walked over to the concrete demarcation line. He pretended to be climbing the symbol of oppression. Sections of the Wall had been left as a reminder to what had been an oppressive communist regime.

Laura snapped a shot of him. The Wall looked to be about twelve feet tall.

"What do you think YBIEN means?" Slam asked as he pointed to a slogan painted in red on the Wall.

"I don't know."

With Laura driving again, they passed the Brandenburg Gate, the entrance to the city. This majestic archway was once closed as it is flush with what was the Berlin Wall. The Reverend Billy Graham held a massive meeting at the Gate shortly after the Wall was dismantled. Tens of thousands of Berliners joined together to hear the world famous evangelist and to thank God for their new freedoms. Laura pointed out the infamous Checkpoint Charlie, one of the once heavily guarded entrances into East Berlin. "They used to push wheeled mirrors under every vehicle to catch anyone clinging to the bottom."

After checking into their hotel, Laura and Slam walked to the Victory Tower. Along the way the trees were green and the flowers were blooming. They passed a park and laughed at some punkish-dressed young people enjoying the wonderful weather.

The Victory Tower celebrates the end of the Franco-Prussian War. They climbed the 285 steps to the top—slowly. There was a great view of the entire city and the Brandenberg Bridge.

Laura and Slam enjoyed a long kiss at the top of the tower—standing next to the angel on top.

While looking toward eastern Berlin, Laura pointed and said, "Do you see that television tower? It is almost 1,200 feet high and the top has a revolving restaurant. When the sun shines on the restaurant, sometimes a cross appears on it. Berliners named the tower the Pope's Revenge." She leaned over and kissed Slam again, amidst the noise of the street traffic below.

Slam liked it. Coca-Cola's accounting problems were far removed from his mind.

Their hotel rooms were so small that Slam had to move two chairs outside their doors in order to open their suitcases.

The next morning, because of jet lag, Slam awoke at 3:30. As they drove out of Berlin they stopped at the 1936 Olympics Stadium. Jesse Owens won his gold medals here. "Der Fuhrer" really fumed when Owens triumphed over members of his "master race" four times. The lush green field was now used mostly for soccer.

By 10:20 Laura and Slam reached what had been the East German border. Soon they were traveling across eastern Germany.

"We'll see few Coke signs in this part of Germany," Laura commented. "Coke was not allowed here when it was East Germany.

Slam's mood turned solemn as he noticed the remnant of high fences left over from the pre-1989 days. Before the political changes, cars were not supposed to stop along the route. It was once a treasonable act for an East German to have an unauthorized contact with a Westerner. Before becoming too solemn, Slam decided to tease Laura.

"Why did Coke have so little success with the former East Germans. Coke still doesn't have a franchise in the Soviet Union. Isn't that an embarrassment? Arch-rival Pepsi is there."

"True, but we're in China, and Pepsi is not. Coke is in at least 160 countries. Coke is one of the world's most popular and best recognized consumer products. More than 60 percent of Coca-Cola's soft drink sales volume is generated outside of the U.S." Laura protested.

Slam could tell that Laura was getting angry, so he changed the subject. "What are you going to do in Warsaw?"

"The name of the game in the nineties is consolidation of resources. By consolidating plants, distribution systems, sales forces, and accounting systems—we can exploit economies of scale. We need to build a 'super plant' in order to spread our costs over the largest feasible number of Cokes."

"I have a meeting with the President of Poland tomorrow to discuss placing a super bottling plant in Poland. As you may know, Poland has the highest birth rate in Europe. I read in some underground literature that reproduction in Poland is an undercover activity." Laura laughed and said, "Maybe it was a Solidarity slogan."

"Where will it be located?" asked Slam.

"Hopefully east of Krakow, near a small town called Oswiecim. It's almost in the center of Europe with railroad tracks leading like spokes throughout Europe."

"Oswiecim. Have I heard that name before?"

"Possibly," Laura nodded. "That's where the Nazis' concentration camp Auschwitz was located. Between 1940 and 1945 more than four million, mainly Jewish, prisoners were gassed or shot by the Nazis and then burned. Of course, you can recognize our public relations problem. We'll have to create another small town near Auschwitz to avoid a possible public outcry. But Hitler selected Oswiecim because of its central location."

"Isn't there an alternate location?" Slam asked.

"Yes. Near Czestochowa. That's the location of a Pauline monastery which houses the holiest shrine in the country—The Black Madonna. Of course, Oswiecim is the best location. Our super plant must be on rail spurs in order to reduce shipping costs."

"Some dilemma," said Slam. "Should Coke pick the best location at the site of the most appalling inhumanity to mankind or pick the lesser location at the center of religious and cultural life of Poland? What spot would the Pope pick?"

"Hey, just south of Oswiecim is Wadowice, the birthplace of Pope John Paul II," smiled Laura.

"Just why are you here?" asked Slam. "You're a computer whiz, not a marketing expert."

"The production facility will be controlled by a black box data processing system. The big computer will run eight to ten lines at high speed. We are talking about 1,600 to 2,000 containers per minute."

"What did Churchill say? Never has so much been delivered to so many by so few." After a few moments Slam continued. "I thought there was an embargo of high-tech computers to former communist countries."

"Very perceptive!" responded Laura. "That's why we're meeting with Lech Walesa tomorrow. He's the same person who negotiated the political agreement for Solidarity in 1989. We must negotiate some type of business agreement to assure the State Department that the big computer will not get into the hands of their military. There's a lot of money made in Poland by-passing the computer embargo."

At Frankfurt-on-the-Oder they crossed the Oder River to go to Poland. They stopped and their passports and visas were checked by a Polish border guard. They filled out a declaration form indicating how much money they were carrying into Poland. Any excess currency of what is entered on the form is subject to confiscation. Also, travelers to Poland must exchange a minimum of $15 per day at the official exchange rate.

Poland, after almost 50 years of Soviet-enforced Marxism-Leninism, is one of the poorest of the Eastern bloc countries. Unstable, with a steadily deteriorating quality of life, its 37 million inhabitants live a grim daily existence. Although Communist-ruled until recently, its citizens are devoutly religious and about 85 percent of the land is privately owned. The Catholic Church is an important force with more than 90 percent of the people Roman Catholics. Even communist oppression could not eradicate Christianity. For that matter, neither could Roman oppression two thousand years earlier.

The road across the flat terrain was in poor condition, and when Laura and Slam turned onto a minor road to a small town named Rezipen, it was narrow, with horse-drawn carts. They had noticed many horses being used in the fields, and the land-owners using sickles to cut their crops.

Rezipen was a little town with about 15,000 people. The quaint, little restaurant served an enjoyable lunch. They started with an appetizer of baked chicken, followed with a bowl of potato soup with mushrooms, a cucumber salad, and sliced tomato. Then came the pork chops, with gravy, potatoes, custard, Coke, and vodka.

"Some lunch," said Slam outside the restaurant.

"You understand, Slam, that food supplies are erratic in Poland," Laura said. "A housewife may spend hours each day in a long line trying to buy food for her family."

Laura saw a little girl sitting on the steps next door to the restaurant. She took her picture, and then gave her a 20 Zoltys coin. The little girl beamed.

Since Warsaw was about 320 miles from the German border, it was about 7:30 when they arrived at the Forum Hotel in Warsaw, the capital of Poland. As they were checking into the hotel, the hotel clerk stamped their visas. Tourists are required to have a stamp on their visas stating where they've slept each night.

After getting their luggage to their rooms, they took a cab to the Old Market restaurant called Kamienne Schodki. Tucked away at the corner of the Old Market, stone stairs descend to the Vistula River which bisects Warsaw.

While waiting for their roast duck, Laura gave Slam a short history of Warsaw. "Poland was the first country attacked by Nazi Germany in 1939. No other city suffered more than Warsaw during WWII. Hitler gave orders to destroy Warsaw. There were four weeks of bombing, and then the German soldiers completely razed the city to the ground. Nothing was left in the systematic destruction, except 45,000 corpses under the ruins. Everything, with clinical precision, was destroyed, street by street with dynamite and petrol. When the army of liberation entered Warsaw in January 1945, not a single human being was alive. Even Hiroshima had *some* survivors. What had taken 700 years to build, the Germans wiped out in less than two months."

"Like a phoenix rising from its ashes," Laura continued, "the Polish people rebuilt the city. This Old Town district was rebuilt exactly as it was before the destruction. The architects used paintings, old prints, and family photographs to rebuild 18th century buildings in this area. You noticed that Old Town is closed to all traffic except horse-drawn cabs."

"Poland is flat, but those large hills we saw as we entered Warsaw are large mounds of the debris carried from the destroyed city. Every citizen became a builder, and a new city came back to life."

After the tasty roast duck, Laura whispered to the waiter when he brought the bill of 620 zoltys, under $4.00 based upon the official rate of exchange. "Will you exchange U.S. dollars?"

"How much?" the waiter asked patiently.

"$40.00," Laura whispered back.

"No problem," replied the smiling waiter.

"What rate?" asked Laura.

"Twice the official rate."

"I can get that with travelers checks. Give me three times the official rate."

"No way. I'll give two and one-half. No more," the waiter replied indignantly.

"Okay," replied Laura, "How?"

"Put the $40 under the napkin, under your bill. I'll take out 620 zoltys, and I'll give you the difference."

Laura followed instructions.

Shortly the waiter returned and left the plate with the zoltys on the table. Laura took the money and left a 400 zoltys tip.

Outside blue-jeaned pedestrians still filled the street and a white-coated soda water ("woda sodowa") vendor stood by his parasoled cart. Slam saw a hot dog vendor fill a roll with dollops of stewed mushrooms from his trailer. He handed the hot dog to a young man dressed in a U.S. Army style jacket.

After a short cab ride back to the Forum and inside her room, Laura counted her money. She then asked Slam, "What's the official exchange rate?"

"About 165 zoltys per one dollar."

"Not bad. I got 15,450 zoltys. But the real black-market or parallel rate is about four times the official rate."

Slam said, "I'll have to exchange some dollars tomorrow like that."

"Be careful; it's illegal to exchange money in the black-market. Do it only with a waiter. The state still has the power of capricious arrest and a long detention without trial. In December, 1981, the military made every telephone in Poland go dead."

Slam thought to himself, "If it's illegal, then why are you doing it, Laura? I think I'll just forget about it!"

★   ★   ★

The next two days for Laura involved a number of meetings with Coca-Cola's employees, Polish governmental officials, and various consultants. The discussions centered around these obstacles:

1. Pros and cons of the two plant locations—Oswiecim or Czestochowa.

2. Ways for Coca-Cola to remove any profits from Poland. Importing and exporting Polish currency is not permitted.

3. The percentage ownership of the participants, Coca-Cola and Poland, in the joint venture.

4. The amount each participant will provide the joint venture.

5. The control of the "super computer" by Coca-Cola in order to convince U.S. officials to allow such a powerful computer in a former communist country.

Lech Walesa attended one of the meetings and did not look like the guy Laura had envisioned. Walesa indicated that he hoped to solve his country's economic and social problems with his free-market economy. But even in his dark-blue suit and red necktie, his ramrod-straight union attitude surfaced when he insisted that the joint venture could take profits out of Poland only if the venture generated hard-currency earnings.

At the end of the second day the Polish government and Coca-Cola issued the following agreement which appeared in *Poityka,* a weekly journal:

> Coca-Cola and Poland have reached a tentative agreement to build a "super" bottling plant in Poland. The location of the plant is still under consideration. Coca-Cola, with a 51 percent stake, will control the joint venture.
>
> A state-of-the-art data processing system will control nine lines at high speeds, to produce 1,800 containers per minute. The profit distributable by the joint venture shall be the excess of its net profit over income tax payable and the required provisions of reserve fund, staff and workers' bonus and welfare fund and enterprise expansion fund. It shall be distributed to the participants of the joint venture in proportion to their shares of contributed capital.
>
> Each participant of the joint venture may audit the accounts of the joint venture. The expenses thereon shall be paid by the participant making the audit. Any problem noted in the audit that needs to be resolved by the joint venture shall be submitted to the joint venture in a timely manner for discussion and resolution.
>
> The assets of the joint venture left over after the clearance of all its debts shall be distributed among the participants of the joint venture according to the proportion of each participant's investment contribution, unless otherwise provided by the agreement, contract or articles of association of the joint venture.

Slam did not attend the two days of meetings but instead checked on the sales account of the major Polish Coca-Cola bottler. He knew that computer data was not a panacea for old fashioned fact checking. On the first morning of his audit he told Laura, "Look, information from a computer data bank is only as good as the person who typed in the original information."

"On one audit I noticed unexplainable swings in sales transactions reported in certain branches. I finally traced the discrepancies to a clerk in Cleveland who occasionally added four zeros to actual figures to ease boredom."

At the bottler's headquarters, Slam found that two clerks verified the quantity, price, and extension of each sales. They then initialed the duplicate invoice to indicate performance. This procedure was a form of internal control. Thus, Slam first performed a compliance audit procedure; he examined a sample of the duplicate sales invoices for the initials of the two women who verified the quantitative data.

Slam found that there were a significant number of documents without a signature. Thus, he had to follow-up with substantive tests. He extended his tests of the duplicate sales invoices by verifying prices, extensions, and footings. In effect, he did a substantive test of the transactions. He found that the invoices *were* correct, because the original clerks preparing the sales invoices had done competent jobs.

Later that evening Slam told Laura that the sales figures for the Polish branch of Coca-Cola were probably correct.

Laura related to Slam the events of her day, and they arranged for wake-up calls at 6:30. Laura wanted to visit the two alternate locations for the future bottling plant.

Chapter 14

Throughout the usual work of accountants, there is the constant pressure to follow the principles of GAAP. Audit procedures are prescribed and due adherence to the rules will produce statements of historical results and current fiscal condition, which meet all the criteria.

— Melvin I. Shapiro, CPA

As they were leaving Warsaw early Wednesday morning, Laura asked Slam, "Do you know the best spot to view Warsaw?"

Without waiting for a response Laura pointed to a tall building. "The best vantage point from which to admire Warsaw is from atop the 37-story Palace of Culture and Science. It's a wedding-cake-sky-scraper gift from Stalin in 1955. That's the only spot in the city from which you can avoid looking at the ugly Stalin-Gothic style."

"I like it," Slam said. "The Wedding Cake building."

"You would," Laura laughed. "The landmark houses museums, theaters, libraries, swimming pools, restaurants, and the Academy of Science. It's the cultural center of Warsaw. We may get to hear a Chopin recital. Chopin was born just outside Warsaw."

Laura negotiated the blue Ford south. She pointed out the fine stucco facades of the 19th century houses. "They are not hidden by commercial signs yet," Laura commented. After leaving Warsaw, she took E82, through Tomaszow Maz and Piotrkow Tryb, toward Czestochowa.

Slam asked, "I've seen a lot of flower peddlers in Warsaw. What's the holiday?"

"No holiday," Laura replied, "There's an age-old Polish tradition of giving flowers on almost any occasion. There are many wealthy farmers who grow roses in glass-covered hothouses."

Horses pulled people in rickety wooden carts along the shoulder of the two-lane road. Farmers pitched hay onto wagons in the fields. There were small fields of barley, wheat, cabbage, and potatoes. Slam noticed the single, box-shaped farmhouses on both sides of the road. Even the huts, however, had a T.V. antenna on top to watch the two state-owned channels. There are more than ten million television sets in Poland—one for every four people. There are VCRs, also. Every few miles Slam saw a cross or a shrine with a figure of the Madonna or Christ, with fresh-cut flowers.

Laura was driving behind a Polish-built Polonez auto as they entered the small town of Czestochowa, the home of the holiest shrine in Poland. "I'm supposed to meet someone at the Dom Pielgrzyma, which is adjacent to the Jasna Gora complex. We're a little early, so let's go to the coffee shop there," she said.

The service was slow, but Laura pulled out an old brochure and started telling Slam about the famous place of pilgrimage for the Poles.

"The object of so many walking pilgrims is Our Lady of Czestochowa, better known as the Black Madonna—not the rock singer in the states. Legend attributes the icon to St. Luke the Evangelist. By the way, Jasna Gora means 'Hill of Light.'"

Laura pointed to the photo in the brochure. "The painting shows Madonna with the Christ child on her left arm. The child is holding a book, known as a *Hogegetria*. The Poles credit the painting for saving their country in 1655. 'Our Lady' gave 230 defenders the strength to repel 4,000 *Protestant* Swedish invaders. The Jasna Gora basilica is Poland's only unconquered fortification."

"What are the two long marks on her right cheek?" Slam asked.

"Again legend states that the scars on her face were inflicted by a would-be Tartar thief who found the icon getting heavier and heavier as he was stealing it. He apparently then fell dead."

Pointing to the photo Slam inquired again, "Why are their faces dark?"

"The original painting may have been from the Fifth century. Thus, some scholars believe it is an exact image of the Virgin Mary; she was a young Jewish woman from Palestine and people from that region were dark."

"Bear in mind," Laura continued, "that the four feet by three feet icon was really completely repainted in 1434 on three repaired cyprus planks from the top of the table of the Holy Family in Nazareth. A woven canvas was glued to the boards and the artists copied the original damaged painting."

Slam read the short description of the painting by the historian Canon Jan Dlugosz of Kracow:

A picture of Mary, the most glorious and the most venerable virgin, the queen of the world and of the Poles, which has been executed with a strange and extraordinary skill, with a serene expression on Her face from whatever direction you look at it. Looking at this picture one is pervaded with a sense of peculiar piety, as if looking at a living person.

"Martin! We are over here." Laura stood up and motioned to a thin, dark-headed person entering the door. When Martin reached the table, Laura shook his hand and said, "Martin Wojdak, I wish you to meet Slam Duncan. Have a seat?" Martin was wearing a Coca-Cola uniform, with an open-neck shirt.

"I can't stay long. I still have some more deliveries to make," Martin replied in heavily accented English.

Laura spoke to Slam. "Martin is probably the only Protestant living in Poland. His great-grandfather was one of the 4,000 Swedish invaders who were repelled by the Poles at Jasna Gora basilica."

"Come on, Laura; don't make up stories. You'll get me in trouble," Martin responded cautiously.

"Don't worry about Slam. How's your son? He's about 13 now, right?"

"Jerzy is only 12. Still thin and tall for his age. My whole family is doing fine." Martin appeared nervous to Slam.

Looking at Slam, Laura said, "Martin drives a Coke truck in this area. He also repairs machinery on the side." Turning back to Martin she asked, "Do you still have to sign a list every morning for two months in order to buy a washing machine in Poland?"

Martin broke his first smile and said, "Yeah, a businessman has many headaches in Poland. I have arranged for you to take a tour of Jasna Gora with a priest who spent some time in the U.S.A. He's going to guide some American tourists at 1:15. Let us walk over and meet him." Martin rose.

Slam took a last sip from his cup of tea, went to pay the bill, but he overheard Laura ask Martin, "Are they in place?"

"Yes, for about four months," was Martin's response in a whisper.

At the monastery Laura and Slam joined a tour group of Americans, most of them accounting students and professors from Texas. They met Fr. Simon Ratynski in the courtyard with the greyish coat-of-arms of the Paulite Order designed into the dirty-white cobblestone. One accounting professor asked Simon, "What type of accounting system does the church use?"

Simon responded smiling, "I'm just a priest." After walking through the Lubomirski Gate, Simon, who spoke excellent English, led the group into the Chapel of Our Lady, through a front door. He took the group of eighteen into the front of the Chapel while a service was proceeding. The Chapel was filled with worshipers singing "Ave Maria." Slam noticed, as he entered, the Baroque stucco decorations in the main part of the interior of the church. There were four side altars and three portals of black marble. The vaulted ceilings were adorned with stucco patterns.

The ebony High Altar contains the Miraculous Picture, surrounded by silver angel ornaments. Above the altar was a pitched canopy of cloth. Slam tried to tiptoe on the black-and-white-marble floor as he moved to get a closer look at the Black Madonna. No photos were allowed.

Slam was able to see the coloration of the Madonna's face with the two scars. The Madonna and Child wore a gown, which was an elaborate overlay of gem-encrusted gold and silver. Before they had entered, Simon indicated that the golden crowns over the heads of the Madonna and child were presented by Pope Pius X in 1910 in connection with the coronation of the icon.

After leaving the Chapel, Simon took the group to a large room with many gifts received by the Paulite Order. Simon merely took a key pinned to his robe and unlocked the wooden door to the room. Slam noticed a simple alarm system attached to the door. There were thousands and thousands of gold and silver items, diamonds, rubies and other precious stones in the glass-encased storage areas. Many wedding and diamond rings, brooches, old coins, tie tacs, and other ornaments were displayed in the large room.

Next Simon took the group to another room where most members bought some souvenirs. Simon was quite a character and an excellent salesperson. Laura bought a Coke from a bright red Coca-Cola machine, and seemed quite pleased. Outside many of the tour members gave Simon a tip, which he readily accepted. One professor got him to pose giving the Aggie sign, an uplifted thumb with clinched fingers. What a sight in Poland, a Polish priest posing with a "good bull" fighting symbol. Shades of Solidarity.

Once Laura and Slam started driving toward Oswiecim, Slam began flipping through the book Laura had bought: *Shrine of the Black Madonna*, by Janusz St. Pasierb.

Almost talking to himself Slam said, "This place has a collection of armour and firearms, musical instruments, portraits, old books and records—Wow! Listen to this. There's a huge gold monstrance. What's a monstrance?"

"That's a vessel in which the consecrated Host is exposed for the veneration of the faithful," Laura spoke calmly.

"Anyway, there's two cloisonne high priests, Melchizedek and Aaron, holding their hands pointing to the Host. The crown has a large diamond, plus 2,366 diamonds, 2,208 rubies, 214 pearls, 81 emeralds, and 30 sapphires." Slam rubbed his finger tips over the glossy picture of the crown in the book.

Slam read for a time while Laura drove in silence. Finally he asked, "Did you know that there are five different robes for the Black Madonna? A ruby robe, a diamond robe—"

"What are the other three robes?" Laura asked quietly.

"I don't know. Can't find it in this book." Slam closed the book with a bang. "I should have bought one of these books."

*   *   *

Their next stop was the Auschwitz concentration camp near Oswiecim. The words on the gate say: Work Brings Freedom. Yet the only way out for four-and-one half years was "through the chimney." The camp has been left as it was found by the Soviets on January 27, 1945 as a grim reminder. From the watch tower at the entrance, Slam and Laura saw the enormity of the largest Nazi death camp. The barracks and crematoria are now museums of the Nazi atrocities, where four million people from 29 nationalities were brought to die after being told they were moving to resettlement areas.

As the people debarked from their train, an S.S. physician determined the fate of the prisoners with either of two words—right or left. About 75 percent of the people were directed straight into the gas chambers—after they removed their clothes. The exhibits showed how progressively efficient the Nazis became. Shooting was too slow, so they built a gas chamber. Slam shivered as he imagined an S.S. efficiency expert moving through the camp making observations and calculations.

There was a huge bin of 5,000 children's shoes, a large bin of false legs, a bin of hair—all being saved by the Nazis to be sent back to the front lines. Gold was removed from corpses' teeth after the gas chamber. The horrible sights and photos of lamps made of skin gave Slam a strange experience of mixed feelings. One exhibit indicated that twins were especially important for the human experiments performed by the S.S. doctors at the camp.

Later outside Laura asked Slam, "Well, can we locate the plant site here?"

Slam breathed slowly and responded, "Ask me tomorrow."

After a short drive to Kracow, the ancient seat of the Polish Kings, Laura and Slam stopped at Orbis-Holiday Inn for the night. Laura spent much of the evening sorting through notes involving the installation of the super computer. Slam noticed that she had Coca-Cola's Accounting Manual open to the section on security over automatic systems.

Slam watched a Polish version of "Grease" on the television as he read a paperback novel. At one point Laura looked up and Slam asked, "Are you a member of the Institute of Internal Auditors?"

"Sure," was Laura's swift response. "I'm a CIA—Certified Internal Auditor. We have standards of Professional Practice like CPAs. Why do you ask?"

"Oh, no reason," Slam responded impassively.

"What are you reading?" Laura asked.

"Oh, a book by Dick Francis called *Risk*. Here, read these two paragraphs." Laura read out loud:

> Although the majority of mankind think of auditing accountants as dry-as-dust creatures burrowing dimly into columns of boring figures, the dishonest regard them as deadly enemies.

> I have had my share of uncovering frauds. I'd lost a dozen people their jobs and set the Revenue onto others, and seen five embezzlers go to prison, and the spite in some of those eyes had been like acid.

She then asked, "English accountant? Right?"

Slam nodded.

Laura went back to work on her CD-ROM reader, which was used to store over 175 separate reference guides, accounting announcements, and software applications. What would fill many bookshelves and weigh hundreds of pounds was now contained on a compact disc weighing less than an ounce. The disc reader was plugged into her microcomputer. She could do research in almost any location now.

After Slam retired to his room for the evening, Laura continued working late into the night. She used the modem on her laptop computer to connect via phone line to her desktop computer back home in Atlanta.

The next morning they drove to the small town of Wieliczka, about eight miles southeast of Kracow, in the sub-Carpathian foothills. Wieliczka has one of the biggest and oldest salt mines in Europe, producing about 700 tons of pure salt a day.

Laura and Slam elected to take an old elevator down the Danilowicz shaft, rather than the 394 step walk. An English-speaking guide met them and six other Americans at the start of the tourist route.

The Polish guide spoke very loudly, "Hello, I am a former salt miner, and I will be your guide for the next two hours! No smoking. Watch your head. Do not touch electric fittings. This salt mine has been in existence for 700 years. There are 20 chambers open to the public along a one-and-a-half mile route. We will descend through three levels to a depth of 442 feet."

"For a long time the sea covered this area, but gradually the sea water evaporated, leaving behind a large quantity of salt. The caves and stalls are reinforced by beams and huge logs. Over the centuries this mine has swallowed vast forests, but fortunately, wood does not rot in a salt-mine. The wood becomes saturated with salt and can last for centuries."

"Miners do not merely dig salt, but some pious miners knew how to carve with salt. Among the carvings you will see today are eight salt gnomes, Holy Cross chapel, methane burners, St. Anton's chapel, Nicolos Copernicus, Princess Kinga, Joseph and Mary with baby Jesus, and a legendary ghost who guards this underground salt-treasure. Follow me and stay close."

The walk underground was fantastic. Along the way in the various chambers and stalls were beautiful statues and reliefs hewed out of the greyish rock salt. The lighting in the subterranean caves made the artwork bright white. Periodically along the way Slam would give Laura a short kiss or put his arm around her. She never protested.

At the underground snack bar most of the group members rested on the wooden benches. At this time the guide told a tall tale about meeting a woman from Chicago. "She has invited me to come visit her in Chicago, so I will accept American dollars as tip."

Laura whispered to Slam. "Do you think he is conning us? They really like hard currency."

After eating ice cream bars and posting some postcards in the underground post office, Laura and Slam continued the tour. The most impressive chamber in the mine was the 180-feet long Chapel of St.

Kinga with octagon-shaped stone flooring. There was a delicate seventeenth-century salt altar, illuminated by five salt chandeliers. Lovely salt statues and bas-reliefs surround the chapel, with a salt version of the Last Supper.

On a lower level were two chambers with two lakes leading to Stanislaw Staszic stall. With a height of 137 feet, the Nazis installed a plant to produce motors for their aircraft during World War II in this chamber. Jewish workers, not miners, were used in this part of the mine. Before the arrival of the Soviet army, the workers were sent to Auschwitz.

After the salt mine tour, Laura and Slam drove back toward Warsaw on E7, passing through Kielce and Radom, to Okecie Airport, about six miles south of Warsaw. Slam had been unexpectedly called back to Atlanta by Lenny. Apparently the professor needed some help with a computer-related problem. Laura planned to travel to Finland and Moscow for a week. They said goodbye at the airport. Slam caught a Lot flight at 6:35 to Frankfurt, connecting with a Pan Am 747 direct flight to Atlanta.

Chapter 15

There are always pivotal questions in the research process. How crucial is the decision? If the wrong decision is made, what will the consequences be?
— David A. Aaker and George S. Day

Lenny was deeply troubled. Some very disturbing findings from his audit investigations had required that he call Slam home from his European travels with Laura. At the moment, however, he simply had to forget his personal concerns and concentrate on his lecture. He looked across the classroom, mentally noting the pre-class activities of his students. Many were talking, some were reading the campus newspaper, and a few were even studying.

He began his lecture. "Today we will examine a critical area of accounting practice, that is, how to effectively research accounting and auditing problems." Most of the students began taking notes.

"The increasingly complex environment facing professional accountants, whether in public practice, industry, or government, often presents problems requiring the in-depth consideration of numerous and complex accounting and auditing issues."

"Accounting and auditing issues are becoming more complex and problems requiring research are being encountered with increasing frequency. While researching tax problems is a normal procedure for many, if not most, practicing accountants, the process of researching accounting and auditing problems is much less familiar."

"The purpose of this lecture is as follows: one, define research; two, discuss the research process; and three, discuss research reference sources; all from the viewpoint of the practicing accountant."

"Research enhances and strengthens the accountant's overall competence and efficiency. It enables the accountant to identify the authoritative, technical information on which sound judgment is based, thus strengthening the accountant's credibility. Research allows the accountant to match the applicable authoritative pronouncements to the accounting and auditing problems encountered."

"In addition to tax, accounting, and auditing services, research is particularly beneficial to the accountant in management consulting engagements. For example, accounting research may be used to identify methods of improving a client's cash flow. It helps the accountant analyze the financial implications of major changes in the client's business operations. Research keeps the accountant, and thus the accountant's clients, up to date on accounting developments and their impact on financial reporting."

"While research is frequently done by accountants in government and industry, accounting and auditing research is especially useful to accountants in public practice. Because of the sheer number and varied backgrounds of their clients, public accounting firms are continually conducting research dealing with a diversity of accounting and auditing issues. The time and resources devoted to research by a number of the larger multi-office firms have led them to establish separate research departments to provide support to the accountants in their everyday work on engagements."

"Research, in general, is an objective, formal process for systematically obtaining, analyzing, and interpreting data for the purpose of providing information useful for decision making. Research may be categorized as pure or applied."

"Pure or basic research may have little or no practical application. Pure accounting research includes the development and testing of new theories of 'how the world works' with respect to accounting practices. Examples of questions asked might include: one, Does the manner in which we as a practice, or as a profession, account for transactions and events make a difference? or two, Does our audit examination and report on the condition of the client's operations make a difference? This type of research, which has little immediate practical application, is often in the form of empirical research, that is, research based on experiment or observation. Pure research is done more by academics, that is, professors, than by practitioners."

"Applied or practical research, the primary subject matter of this lecture, deals with the analysis of a particular question or problem of immediate practical concern. For example, a client may be considering the acquisition of new plant equipment and may wish to know the effects this acquisition will have on the financial statements. If the client seeks the accountant's advice before the transaction occurs, then the accountant conducts *a priori*, before the fact, research. Research regarding a completed transaction is referred to as *a posterior*, after the fact."

"For the practitioner, applied or practical research may be described as a logical process of acquiring and documenting evidence supporting a conclusion regarding an accounting or auditing issue or problem. Properly documenting the research process is a basic and essential characteristic of good research."

"Both pure and applied research are essential to the accounting profession. Applied research is obviously necessary to solve the practical problems encountered in everyday practice. It is related to the technical competence the business community expects from the accounting profession. Pure research contributes to the overall body of accounting knowledge and, hopefully, will eventually be of assistance in solving practical problems."

A student's hand being raised captured Lenny's attention. "Yes," he responded. "What's your question, Randy?"

Randy Dumas was one of Lenny's favorite students. Randy usually asked thoughtful questions that were not easily answered. Lenny enjoyed interacting with all of his students, but he particularly appreciated feedback from students like Randy.

"Is this a 'publish or perish' school, Dr. Cramer?" Without waiting for a response, Randy continued, "Do you like teaching or research the most?" Most of the students looked up from their note-taking.

Although Cramer was a little surprised by the personal nature of Randy's inquiries, he tried to look impassive as he replied. "Those are two good questions, Randy. My lecture, as I've previously indicated, is chiefly concerned with practitioner research, rather than a professor's research; thus, your questions are a little off the subject. However, I will answer them anyway." A few students chuckled.

"Regarding your first question, virtually all schools expect some research activity from their faculties. I believe research is important because it helps professors stay up-to-date and enthusiastic about recent developments in the accounting field. Consequently, professors can do a better job teaching by being involved in some research. Regarding your second question, I always give my students' problems priority over my research projects. I consider teaching and counseling students more important than research, but as I've indicated, some research is necessary."

147

Cramer paused. He asked, "Does anyone else have a question?" When no one responded, he resumed his lecture.

"The fundamental steps in the research process include the following: problem identification, planning the research, gathering evidence, evaluating evidence, and drawing a conclusion. Problem identification is the initial step in the research process. For example, a client may ask the accountant to determine the impact of a particular transaction. Usually, further refinement of the precise problem is necessary. The practitioner must identify the problem as specifically as possible, to avoid wasting time and effort reviewing sources which are not relevant to the specific issues under consideration. The starting point for effective research is a clear identification of the problem."

"The second step in the research process is planning a specific strategy for carrying out and completing the research. Three components are included in planning the research project. The first is an overview of the accounting or auditing problem under consideration. This overview includes a statement of the research objectives and research questions to be answered. Second, the research methodology is identified: a) data to be collected; b) procedures to be used in collecting the data; and, c) techniques to be used in analyzing the data. Finally, the researcher's resources, principally time, are allocated and scheduled."

"Once the problem is clearly identified and a research plan is developed, the practitioner is ready to gather the appropriate evidence. This step typically includes a detailed review of relevant authoritative accounting and/or auditing literature, as well as a survey of current practice. The primary sources of authoritative accounting literature are as shown."

Cramer paused to place an overhead transparency on the projector. The projector displayed the following information.

Highest level of accounting authority:

1. Non-superseded sections of the Accounting Research Bulletins issued by Committee on Accounting Procedures

2. Non-superseded sections of the APB Opinions issued by the Accounting Principles Board

3. Statements of Financial Accounting Standards issued by the FASB

4. Interpretations issued by the FASB

5. Statements and Interpretations of the Governmental Accounting Standards Board (for governmental units)

Next level of accounting authority:

1. AICPA Industry Accounting Guides
2. AICPA Statements of Position
3. FASB and GASB Technical Bulletins
4. Industry accounting practices
5. AICPA Accounting Interpretations

Lower level of accounting authority

1. Guidelines published by SEC and other regulatory agencies
2. FASB and GASB Concept Statements
3. APB Statements
4. AICPA Issues Papers
5. Minutes of the FASB Emerging Issues Task Force
6. Other professional association statements
7. Accounting textbooks, reference books, and articles written by recognized authorities in the field

"The literature with the highest level of accounting authority is designated by Rule 203 of the AICPA *Code of Professional Ethics* as '...accounting principles promulgated by the body designated by Council to establish such principles ...' The FASB is the source presently designated to promulgate accounting principles. If a transaction or event is not covered under Rule 203, then AU Section 411 provides further guidance in determining the acceptable accounting treatment."

"Auditing standards issued by the AICPA's Auditing Standards Board, that is, the ASB, comprise the literature having the highest level of auditing authority, derived from Rule 202 of the AICPA's *Code of Professional Ethics*. Also, the Auditing Standards Division issues periodic Auditing Interpretations to provide guidance in the use of the standards issued by the ASB. While these Interpretations do not have the authority of auditing standards, they are reviewed by members of the ASB and carry the caveat that if the quality of a practitioner's work is questioned, then AICPA members must justify any departures from an Interpretation."

"Additionally, the Auditing Standards Division issues *Statements of Position* to revise or clarify recommendations included in audit guides. As is the case with Interpretations, AICPA members may be required to justify departures from *Statements of Position*. Industry accounting and auditing guides are provided by committees of the AICPA and are subject to the approval of senior technical committees."

Cramer stopped lecturing to replace the initial overhead transparency with a second one. The second transparency included the following information.

Highest auditing authority:

1. Statements on Auditing Standards issued by the ASB
2. Auditing Interpretations issued by the Auditing Standards Division
3. AICPA Code of Ethics
4. Industry Audit Guides
5. Statements of Position issued by the Auditing Standards Division
6. GAO Standards for governmental audits

Lower auditing authority:

1. Audit Research Monographs
2. AICPA Audit and Accounting Manual
3. Auditing textbooks, reference books, and articles written by recognized authorities in the field

Cramer continued his lecture. "Since the sources of authority differ between accounting and auditing, it is essential that the researcher distinguish whether the problem under consideration is primarily accounting or auditing-oriented. Otherwise, the researcher may waste valuable time searching inappropriate sources."

"Accounting has been defined as '...the art of recording, classifying, and summarizing in a significant manner and in terms of money, transactions and events which are in part at least, of a financial character, and interpreting the results thereof.' The major objective of accounting is to extract relevant decision-making information from a firm's information system, and provide this data to internal users, that is, management, and to external users, such as investors, government, and others."

"Auditing, on the other hand, is a different process. Auditing has been defined as follows: '... a systematic process of objectively obtaining and evaluating evidence regarding assertions about economic actions and events to ascertain the degree of correspondence between those assertions and established criteria and communicating the results to interested users.'"

"Auditing, the attest function, aids the users of accounting information by evaluating the quality of the information presented. Auditing considers business events and conditions, but does not encompass the tasks of measuring or communicating accounting issues for propriety. Auditing is primarily analytical, rather than constructive; it is investigative in nature. Auditing concerns proof, the basis for financial statements. Auditing concepts and methodology are founded less on accounting principles, and more on the general principle of logic."

"The fourth major step in the research process consists of evaluating evidence gathered from the authoritative literature and identifying alternative actions. During this process, tentative conclusions may be drawn. If alternative actions are not supported by precise rules found in the authoritative literature, then actions should be theoretically justified. It may be necessary to conduct additional research regarding alternative actions. This research may include consultation with colleagues, as well as further discussions with the client. Naturally, the researcher must remain objective throughout the process and keep in mind that the client may be biased."

"Following the detailed analysis of each alternative action, the researcher arrives at a logical conclusion. This conclusion should be well-documented and based on the evidence gathered. The conclusion is ultimately presented to the client as the proposed solution to the problem."

A student sitting near the back of the classroom did not raise her hand, but asked, "What if the client doesn't like the auditor's solution?"

"That's a dilemma," Cramer replied. "If they can't resolve their differences, then the auditor may have to withdraw from the engagement."

Cramer resumed his lecture. "In deriving the conclusion, the accountant or auditor frequently employs his or her professional judgment. Opinions of other professionals also may be consulted. Several published sources enable the practitioner to determine how others have dealt with particular accounting and reporting issues. These include the following."

"The first is *Technical Practice Aids* which is published by the AICPA. This service includes inquiries and responses describing actual problems encountered in practice. The response includes the interpretation and recommendations, as well as the relevant standards and authoritative sources. The AICPA also provides guidance in handling audit and accounting problems through its technical Hotline. This hotline service, including the phone call, is free to all AICPA members."

"The second is *Accounting Trends & Techniques* which is published annually by the AICPA. It illustrates current reporting practices."

"The third is *National Automated Accounting Research System*, or simply NAARS, which is maintained by the AICPA. NAARS is a full-text, computerized information retrieval system. It includes the annual reports of over 4,200 publicly-held corporations. NAARS also includes all current and superseded authoritative and semi-authoritative literature from the AICPA, FASB, GASB, and the SEC."

"A number of useful reference services are available to assist the practitioner in locating authoritative sources. These reference services include: one, AICPA Professional Standards; two, FASB Accounting Standards; three, AICPA Index to Accounting and Auditing Technical Pronouncements; four, AICPA Technical Practice Aids; five, The Accountant's Index and the AICPA Library; and six, Computerized Information Retrieval Services, such as NAARS. These services assist the practitioner in remaining current regarding pronouncements, interpretations, and guidelines concerning today's complex practice environment."

"The creation of the *AICPA Professional Standards* loose-leaf subscription service in 1974 established an excellent research resource for use by professional accountants. The loose-leaf service consists of two volumes; Volume 1 contains the U.S. Auditing Standards (SASs and Auditing Interpretations) while Volume 2 has eight major divisions."

"The *Professional Standards* features a topical index. For example, if the researcher has a question concerning auditors' opinions, the index under 'U.S. Auditing' in the *Professional Standards*, may be consulted rather than scanning all the SASs and Interpretations. In addition to this index, each volume includes a number of helpful appendices. For example, an appendix in the U.S. Auditing section lists the industry audit guides."

"There has been some confusion regarding the use of the *Professional Standards*. It includes section numbers in place of original pronouncement numbers. For example, SAS No. 39, 'Audit Sampling', is listed as AU Section 350. The use of section numbers facilitates indexing. The indexing system provides for referencing specific sections within a section. For example, AU Section 350.03 refers to the third paragraph of Section 350. Also, the Auditing Interpretations are numbered in the 9000's, and the last three numbers specify the SAS section to which the Interpretation relates. For example, AU Section 9642 indicates that the Interpretation concerns AU Section 642."

"The FASB Accounting Standards consists of two volumes. The first volume is the *Original Pronouncements* which includes the unabridged original text of AICPA Accounting Research Bulletins; APB Opinions and Interpretations; and a companion volume of FASB Statements of Standards, Statements of Concepts, Interpretations and Technical Bulletins. The *Original Pronouncements* also provide background information comments by dissenting Board members, and the basis for conclusions. This information may be important at times to have a complete understanding of the impact of the pronouncement."

"The second volume includes the *Current Text* which presents key material from the 'Original Pronouncements' arranged in the format of a dictionary or encyclopedia. Subjects are arranged alphabetically in two major divisions: general standards and industry standards."

"The AICPA Index to Accounting and Auditing Technical Pronouncements enables the researcher to rapidly locate the professional standards, official pronouncements, and technical guides that affect accounting and auditing questions. This reference service includes all authoritative materials issued by the AICPA, FASB, GASB, SEC, International Accounting Standards Committee, International Federation of Accountants, CASB, and National Council on Governmental Accounting."

"The AICPA Technical Practice Aids contains authoritative examples and commentary. It consists of two volumes. Volume 1 includes the Technical Information Service, or TIS, a compilation of practical questions and responses. This compilation is organized by major topic areas, including: financial statement presentation, assets, liabilities and deferred credits, capital, revenue and expense, special industry problems, special organizational problems, audit field work, and audit reports."

"Volume 2 of the *Technical Practice Aids* includes: one, Statements of Position, of the Accounting Standards Division and the Auditing Standards Division; two, *Practice Bulletins* of the Accounting Standards Executive Committee; three, *Issues Papers* of the Accounting Standards Division; and, four, a Voluntary Quality Control Review Program."

"The Accountant's Index provides a summary of new publications in accounting, tax, and management advisory services. Publications are indexed by both author and topic area. The AICPA Library houses books and journals relating to auditing, accounting, financial reporting, financial management, investments and securities, data processing, taxation, management, and related topics. These books and journals are available for loan to AICPA members."

"Numerous computer data bases are currently available for the use of researchers. During the period, 1979 to 1988 alone, the number of data bases increased from 400 to 3,893 in the *Directory of Online Data Bases*."

"Computerized databases, such as NAARS, are expected to become increasingly useful research tools for the practicing accountant. The expanding volume of data that impacts accounting and auditing issues may be manipulated and searched more efficiently in a computerized database. The computerized information retrieval services that have been discussed provide the busy practitioner with ready access to business-related databases."

"The professional library of every practitioner should include several basic reference volumes. A number of basic reference sources have already been identified and discussed; however, there are additional sources which may be of assistance to the practitioner in his or her research efforts. The AICPA publication, *Management of an Accounting Practice Handbook*, includes a list of publications to guide the practitioner in establishing a basic reference library. Selected items from this list are as shown."

Cramer once again stopped to place an overhead transparency on the projector. The following information was displayed.

BASIC REFERENCE LIBRARY

1. Official Pronouncements and Interpretations of AICPA Senior and Technical Committees:
   a) *Professional Standards*
   b) *Industry Accounting and Audit Guides*

2. FASB *Financial Accounting Standards*

3. SEC Accounting Releases (ASRs, FRRs, and AAERs) and Regulation S-X.

4. General References: Various nonauthoritative reference books, including handbooks, manuals, and guides.

5. Tax Services: The AICPA recommends subscription to at least one federal income tax loose-leaf service.

6. AICPA Publications (partial list):
   a) *Accountants' Index*
   b) *Accounting Trends & Techniques*
   c) *Audit and Accounting Manual*
   d) *Financial Report Surveys*
   e) *GAAP for Smaller and/or Closely Held Businesses*
   f) *Index to Accounting and Auditing Technical Pronouncements*
   g) *Management Advisory Services by CPAs*
   h) *Management Advisory Services Guidelines Series*
   i) *Management of an Accounting Practice Handbook*
   j) *Statements of Position* of the Accounting Standards Division
   k) *Statements on Standards for Accounting and Review Services*
   l) *Technical Practice Aids*

7. Periodicals and Newsletters (partial list):
   a) *Accounting Review* (American Accounting Association)
   b) *CPA Letter* (AICPA)
   c) *Journal of Accountancy* (AICPA)
   d) *Management Accounting* (National Association of Accountants)
   e) *Practical Accountant* (Institute for Continuing Professional Education)
   f) *The CPA Journal* (New York State Society of CPAs)

"A critical attribute of the accounting or auditing researcher is that he or she keeps informed and current as to the latest developments in the field. The accounting practitioner must remain up-to-date regarding authoritative developments, as well as other issues and developments

155

affecting the business environment. The reference sources previously discussed are extremely useful in this process."

A student interrupted. "Professor Cramer, let's get real! How can anyone possibly keep up with all this material? Are accountants supposed to be like Superman or something?" The question resulted in considerable laughter from the class.

"No one expects us to have all this information memorized, but we have to know how to find the pertinent information when we face a problem. In any case, the business community, not to mention the government, expects a professional level of service from the accounting profession. To maintain confidence in the profession, it is essential that accountants, particularly those in public practice, understand and effectively utilize research."

Lenny looked at his Cartier watch. The time was close to the end of the class period. Consequently, he knew there would be no responses, but he asked anyway, "Does anyone have any further questions before we dismiss?"

The students began closing their books and preparing to leave. Cramer said, "Okay, I'll see you next time." With that remark, the students quickly filed out of the room. Lenny, left alone, and weary from his lecture, plopped down in a desk. In less than an hour he had to leave for the airport to pick up Slam. Slam would be surprised at what the Coke audit had uncovered.

Chapter 16

Coke is it!

Once the alarm system was compromised, the thin figure took off a ski mask, gloves, and a heavy coat. He put the gloves back on as he walked toward a Coca-Cola machine. Only after drinking a Classic Coke and eating some peanut butter crackers did the silent figure go to work.

Taking a crowbar the dark intruder broke into a treasure room and moved to the nearest glass-enclosed case. He placed a large flashlight face down on the glass and turned it on. Next a large suction cup was placed on top of the glass, and a round circle was cut with a glass cutter in the glass. After placing the round glass on the floor, his gloved hands placed the jewelry and other precious items into a brown cloth sack. Methodically the prowler emptied nineteen other glass-enclosed cases. When a sack was full, he took the full sack and placed it into the secret compartment.

After the remaining eleven storage cases were emptied, the thief broke into another storage room. The diamonds on the Diamond Robe sparkled as the light of his flashlight hit them. It disappeared into a cloth sack. Two other gem-encrusted gowns were placed on top of the Diamond Robe. Like Santa Claus on the night before Christmas, the robber placed the heavy sack over his shoulder and carried it back to a second secret compartment. This second hiding place was almost full, so the thin prowler became more selective on his return to the storage room.

He decided against taking the reliquary of St. Paul the Hermit—no gems on it. But his small hands gently placed the reliquary of the Holy Cross into his cloth sack. He liked the very large blue stone on it. He softly counted the number of precious stones on a crosier showing the Holy Trinity. There were 22 rubies and two large sapphires. Another chalice had 10 rubies, 6 emeralds, and at least 4 unknown white stones.

157

A statue of an angel was too heavy; so also was a tray with a garden scene.

Forget about a 17th century goblet, a tray for ampullae, a plate with a scene of the annunciation, and two candlesticks. But he took one of two vases—he liked the eight big green stones—and one of three flint muskets. The last item placed into his sack was a monstrance with a golden crown on top. After dragging the sack back to the secret compartment, he found that the sack would not fit. He pulled out the monstrance, closed the door, and wrapped the monstrance in another sack. He placed the sack next to the Coca-Cola machine, and began drinking another Coke.

He had not found the Ruby gown. "It must be on the Black Madonna," he thought. He walked to the storage area, and put a rosary and a golden chain into his pockets. Then he walked into the library, and shined his flashlight onto the white polychrome ceiling painting. He rested in a large armchair with the coat-of-arms of the Paulite Order. "Not comfortable," he said softly.

Retracing his steps, he began picking up his equipment—suction cup, glass cutter, ski mask, and the heavy coat. "Wait a minute." He put everything down, and walked over and retrieved the two Coke crates. After placing them next to the drink machine, he put on his coat, and stuffed the ski mask into his right coat pocket. He picked up the sack with the monstrance, walked over to the window next to the door, and cut a round hole in it. He then opened the window, climbed out, shut the window, and placed the round piece of glass on the ground. Cautiously he made his way through the Lubomirski Gate, across the courtyard, and disappeared into the still morning darkness. In forty more minutes the sun would shine on the Shrine of the Black Madonna.

*   *   *

Not until the second day after the burglary did it become public. A spokesperson for the Polish Catholic church indicated that there had been a significant robbery at the Jasna Gora Monastery. A reward of two million zoltys was offered for the recovery of the stolen sacred artifacts. The spokesperson assured the world that the priceless Black Madonna was safe.

An official of the Polish Communist party stated that the robbery probably had been planned by a few Solidarity members to help improve Poland's economic situation. A Kremlin official indicated that many Catholics suspected the "irresponsible hand of the CIA" in the "breaching of the security system" at the holy shrine. The State Department denied any knowledge of the unfortunate theft and offered any U.S. aid in recovering the stolen religious treasures.

A spokesman for Lech Walesa said that the desperados would be found and punished. Many of the underground newspapers began carrying the following account of the robbery. "The bandits might have had inside help because the alarm system was off during the entry into the monastery. The only other logical conclusion is that someone forgot to switch on the silent alarm system (a highly coincidental accident). Or else the alarm system was faulty, which an official of the Paulite Order denied."

Another newspaper indicated that the Diamond Robe, two other gowns, and the priceless "Aaron and Melchizedek" monstrance were part of the stolen artifacts. The robbers apparently made no attempt to take the Black Madonna, who fortunately was wearing the Ruby Robe.

Chapter 17

Following the high incidence of defective and error prone systems, data and asset mishandling, and fraud, there is a great need for all concerned to learn how to secure, control, and audit computerized systems by prescribing effective controls to prevent, detect, and correct errors, minimize system improprieties, and protect data.

— Michael J. Cerullo

Laura was participating in perestroika—the restructuring of the Soviet economy. Yes, *glasnost*—or public openness or democratization—was more evident now than on her last trip to the Soviet Union four years ago. This week Laura was participating in a Finnish seminar dealing with the "Soviet Union as a Business Partner."

The first three days of the seminar had taken place in Helsinki, Finland. The Finnish Export Institute suggests that Helsinki is the gateway to the USSR. Located in the northernmost corner of Europe between Sweden and the Soviet Union, Finland is the home of Santa Claus, saunas, and reindeer meat. Laura was told that much business was transacted in saunas, but she did not ask if there were many female business executives in Finland.

So far the seminar was interesting, covering the Soviet economic system, joint ventures, Soviet negotiating, and practical advice. With perestroika, the Soviet Union was pushing joint ventures between Soviet and foreign partners. A joint venture is not part of the planned system, so it functions as an absolutely independent production unit answerable for all its operations exclusively with its own resources.

Another way of dealing with the Soviet Union was through a buyback agreement. Since roubles are worthless outside of the USSR, the major problem is how to get profits out of the country. For example, for many years Pepsi-Cola Company took its profits out in the form of vodka. Since the Soviets prefer to trade goods for goods because of their deficit of foreign currency, Pepsi signed a deal to trade Pepsi-Colas, pizzas, and Kentucky Fried Chicken for 85 ships worth nearly $2.6 billion.

Things really had changed in the Soviet Union due to Mikhail Gorbachev's *glasnost*. The October 1989 Moscow Book Fair featured an American stand run by the Evangelical Christian Publishers Association (ECPA). Muscovites lined up in hundreds to get one of the 10,000 copies of the New Testament being provided for free. Near the ECPA stand was a completely empty one run by the American Atheist Press Inc. It was rather obvious that the Russian people already knew enough about atheism. Thanks to new import rules, the West helped bring in more than a million copies of the Bible in one year; although the *Wall Street Journal* reported that was far short of the demand.

Laura thought about a conversation she had with Lenny just before the trip. Lenny told her of the amazing new openness at universities in the Soviet Union. In 1989, the university in Tbilisi, the capital city in the Soviet Republic of Georgia, invited a group of professors to lecture audiences of professors and students about the relevance of Christianity to the academic world. Coinciding with the lecture series, the film, "JESUS" was shown at the Tbilisi Philharmonic Hall. Since its U.S. debut in 1979, the film had been shown to more than 330 million people in over 160 countries. It had been dubbed into more than 140 languages, including the Georgian language.

One of the lecturers, Dr. William Jordan, Associate Professor of Mechanical Engineering at Louisiana Tech University, traced the origins of science and discussed the Christian faith of many of the early scientists, such as Galileo. Dr. Jordan concluded his talk with a personal testimony and emphasized that he believed there was no conflict between faith and science. Dr. Jordan's translator, "an admitted atheist," told Jordan, "You are the first person to talk about God in our institution in 70 years."

Laura had been slightly shocked when she arrived at the best hotel in Moscow, the Mezhdunarodnaja, from the Moscow airport. The modern hotel looked like a Hyatt Regency, with a large open inside area with five glass elevators serving thirteen floors. Inside the lobby was a bright red Coke machine—Ko-Ka Kora. Of course, it took her about 20 minutes to purchase a token for one dollar to obtain a real Coke. The machine was serviced by a German firm.

There was a round American Express money machine and advertising inside the large, open lobby. Advertising occurred even in the heart of a communist country. There was a large sign for the British-Soviet Chamber of Commerce, Pan Am, Wesotra (a transportation association), and BNL (an Italian Bank). Laura reminded herself that only foreigners were allowed in an intourist hotel—not Soviet citizens. The shops in the hotel took only hard currency and not Soviet roubles.

Laura walked on the white tile floor to look at one of the many birch trees inside the lobby. The trunk of the tree was real, but the branches and leaves were fake. There were bright maroon carpets, chairs, and round tables around a water fountain with several large pools containing large red fish.

There was a large, wooden-like clock seven stories high with a rooster on top. While Laura was checking into the hotel, the rooster began to crow on the hour, flapped its wings, and two wooden men began blowing their horns. What a sight.

Jet lag caused Laura to awake at 5:30 on Friday morning, so she decided to write Slam. She knew the letter would arrive later than her flight back on Saturday evening, but she wanted to determine how long an express mail letter would take.

Dear Great One,

I'm looking out of the 12th floor, room 1241 in the best Moscow hotel. I can see a large river, smoke stacks, pollution, and one of the eight Stalin buildings, called the wedding cake. About 6:30.

Most buildings are dull red brick with some yellowish brick. Very little traffic on the road at this time. No boat traffic, but one boat called the Rivera is tied up at a pier.

All is fine. The conference is a success. I saw Red Square and the Cathedral of St. Basil yesterday. Also went to Gum Department Store.

Dull smoggy sky. I have yet to really see the sun. Truly polluted here. Red buoys in the middle of the river. There are colored cars—red, white, light green, and blue. Trucks are no longer military green. I see some typical 18 wheelers parked outside on the street.

My room is reasonably large. Wall paper. Lamps. TV. Two single beds. Bathroom works. Actually it's a surprisingly large room with a round end table. Two large, stuffed chairs (brown), table for TV, with a longer table with a cloth straight-back chair.

I'll be back Saturday evening. I'll check out their express postal service. Long live U.S.A.

Love Laura

After the seminar, Laura went with the group of eighteen Americans to the famous round Bolshoi Theatre to see a Polish ballet. The stately and brightly decorated interior had six rows of red velvet upholstery and gilded boxes with sparkling cutglass chandeliers. The frieze in front had red flags and two images of Lenin. There were many figures of people on the round ceiling.

The ballet was shocking by Moscow atheist standards. It was a bizarre, *avant-garde* ballet with many symbols. There was Christ ascending into heaven, Mary at a tombstone, and flying nuns. Laura first thought that a very loud scene was a UFO landing, but it was instead the bombing of Poland in World War II. There was little clapping from the audience, and a number of people left early. One businessman joked that many of the Marx/Lenin people left early in disgust.

★   ★   ★

"What a boring movie and flight," thought Laura Lee Bertone on her flight from New York to Atlanta. She was thinking about all the fun she had missed during her fast-paced twenty-six years. She had been so busy with work, particularly in the computer area, that she had had little time for romance— until Slam Duncan had wandered into her life.

When the plane landed, she wished someone would be there to greet her at the "Big Hustle" airport terminal. Funny. Atlanta's biggest employer is the airport. But she knew there would be no one there. This business trip had been hectic. She really wished Slam had not been called back early by *that* Professor Cramer. Slam would have made the return trip much more enjoyable. She would really be glad when Cramer's operational audit was finished. Then Slam would have more time to spend with her.

Laura was extravagant by nature. She considered herself very cultured. She liked good food, wine, nice clothes, and when she traveled she liked to go first class. She was independent, so where did Slam fit in? She was perplexed.

The plane taxied around the Hartsfield International Airport an insufferably long time after landing—even for Atlanta. Finally, the passengers were told they could disembark. As usual, many people had already stood up to get their carry-on bags, before the plane came to a complete stop at the terminal. She never stood until permission came over the speaker.

As she walked from the plane she spotted Duncan in the crowd. She smiled at this pleasant surprise. "How sweet," she thought, "he's come to the airport to welcome me home. Perhaps I should be more honest with him?"

Slam's gray eyes met hers. They were cold. He wasn't smiling. "What's wrong," she thought. Now they were only a few feet away from each other. Suddenly she noticed two Atlanta cops standing beside Slam.

"That's her," he said sadly.

Her heart was in her throat. She could not take a breath. Her mind raced with thoughts. "They can't know. Slam, Slam, what have you done?" She felt the policemen's hands grab her shoulders. She did not resist. One of the policemen told her her rights. It seemed like a dream—no, a waking nightmare. A shudder came over her. As they escorted her to the police car, she looked over at Slam. He would not look at her. "Was that a look of anguish on his face?"

After driving her to the downtown police station, she was taken to an interrogation room. Slam came into the small room. The officers left and locked the door, leaving Slam and her alone.

"Don't you see?" he asked. "You're finished! We're finished!" He sat down hard in one of the wooden, straight-back chairs.

"Slam, I love you." She choked on the words.

"No matter," Slam said painfully. "While we were in Poland, Lenny cracked the case. He asked me to fly home early to prepare me for this wonderful reunion. He was afraid you might try to frame me and drag me down with you. I didn't believe him at first, but then he showed me evidence of what you've been doing."

He looked sternly into Laura's eyes.

"The night after we left on our trip, Lenny used the electronic spying equipment that I originally purchased to tap Loebbecke's computer. I thought Loebbecke was our Coke culprit. Lenny thought

Loebbecke was too obvious. Turns out Lenny was right. He had a hunch that your computer knowledge would make it possible for you to pull off the Coke computer system shenanigans. But what really tipped him off was when he discovered you had worked with Loebbecke before he retired from Coke. You probably learned his computer password at that time and used it to throw us off your trail. You clandestinely entered the Coke computer system using a Trojan Horse program. I can't determine whether you wrote the program or simply discovered it. No matter. We got rid of it."

"To make a long story short, Lenny parked in front of your apartment and recorded images from your computer. Using a modem on each end, you used your laptop computer in Poland to dial into your desktop microcomputer back home in Atlanta. You then examined the inventory records, and the Coke formula you had derived from those records. You even made the mistake of sending messages offering the formula for sale over your computer's modem to several people in India. Lenny has it all on video tape."

"What! How?" Her face paled.

Slam ignored her question. "You knew that India tried to obtain the Coke formula many years ago. When Coke would not disclose the secret formula, India kicked Coke out of the country. India replaced Coke with a similar looking soft drink. Apparently the cloned cola doesn't taste too good. You decided to sell the formula to your contacts in India for four million dollars. Not bad pay for a data processor."

"Okay, so you know how I figured out the Coke formula. Is that illegal? You can't prove I tried to sell it. All you have is circumstantial evidence. Someone else may have been using my computer to send messages."

"Laura, it's over. Why don't you just give up? We also know you're the one who masterminded the theft of artifacts from the Jasna Gora religious site. While you were on your return plane trip, the Polish police arrested Martin Wojdak. He immediately confessed how you arranged for him to be the driver to service the Coke machines at Jasna Gora. Four months ago, working together, y'all had those specially reconstructed machines placed at the site. I overheard you ask him 'Are they in place?'"

Laura looked totally shattered, but said nothing.

Slam continued. "Lenny discovered that sales were down dramatically after the old drink machines were replaced. The declining sales stuck out like a sore thumb on the monthly sales reports. Why would sales decline due to new machines? After the Poland theft made the papers a few days ago, Cramer figured it might be related to those Coke machines. He called the Poles. They checked out the drink machines. Most of the religious artifacts were found in the two secret compartments in the backs of the machines. The police then apprehended Wojdak at home. He had already taken a few items to his house, and there was no way he could deny the theft. Naturally, he didn't try to protect you. In fact, he claims you blackmailed him to do it. He says you threatened to fire him if he didn't help you."

"He's lying. You can't prove anything!" Laura shouted.

"Laura! Shut up! We know everything! The police obtained a search warrant for your apartment. While looking for anything connected to the Poland robbery, they found some white powder hidden in a bag in the back of your closet. They were surprised when it was not identified as cocaine! I wasn't. The voodoo powder is now just one more item in the stack of evidence against you. Laura, you murdered an innocent student and you nearly killed me!"

Laura tried to interrupt, but Slam continued.

"So far I haven't been able to break into all your computer files, but eventually I will. And when I do, I suspect I'll find a program that sends subliminal messages about flying."

"Slam, you must believe me," she pleaded. "The Zombie powder wasn't supposed to kill you, just scare you off. I don't know why that student died. He must have had a bad reaction. And I don't know anything about subliminal messages!"

Slam stood up slowly and said, "I can't believe a word you say. I loved you once, but that's over."

Laura looked into Slam's eyes. When their eyes met, she thought his gaze would burn a hole through her. She had to turn away. She was more afraid than ever before in her life. She had lost everything.

With a shake of his head, Slam turned and walked quickly out of the room. He decided to go back to work on his dissertation. Writing about expert systems was certainly safer than auditing Coca-Cola.

The front page bold headline in the *Atlanta Constitution* on Thursday proclaimed: "Black Madonna Trips Programmer's Scheme." A copyrighted story by Hugh Nations began as follows:

> Black Madonna was almost ripped off by Ms. Laura Lee Bertone, a computer whiz working for Coca Cola. She attempted to steal artifacts from the Jasna Gora, the religious site of the Black Madonna. This high-achieving

employee almost pulled it off with the help of two Coca-Cola machines with false-backs.

Aside from the millions to be earned from the theft of the artifacts, Laura Lee Bertone, almost sold the Coca-Cola formula to certain individuals from India for $4 million. Two alert forensic accountants stopped both schemes by checking accounting records prepared in Poland. Dr. Lenny Cramer, at Georgia State University and Mr. Beauregard (Slam) Duncan—

*   *   *

Educators who teach auditing have a responsibility to prepare students for microcomputer audit applications by requiring their use in the auditing course. In many cases the educator must try to meet this responsibility with limited resources relative to facilities, time, and expertise.
— Robert E. Guinn